"Is Darrin the one shooting at us?" Harry asked.

Eyes wide with fear, Ramona nodded.

The men tromped through the forest toward them. They couldn't stay here. They'd be found.

He gestured at Ramona to stay quiet, then pressed his phone and truck keys into her hand. He leaned toward her, speaking close to her ear. "My truck is parked on the road. Run for it and drive out of here as fast as you can. The cops are already on their way."

"What about you?" she asked.

"I'll lead them in the other direction."

She hesitated, so he gave her a little push. But before either of them could get moving, Harry heard the sound of several vehicles pulling up to a stop on the highway near where he'd parked.

"Cops!" one of the men in the forest yelled.

"This isn't over, Ramona!" Darrin called out. "You better make sure you keep your mouth shut! If you don't, I'll find you. I'll make sure you and your whole family keep their mouths shut. *For good!*"

Jenna Night comes from a family of Southern-born natural storytellers. Her parents were avid readers and the house was always filled with books. No wonder she grew up wanting to tell her own stories. She's lived on both coasts but currently resides in the Inland Northwest, where she's astonished by the occasional glimpse of a moose, a herd of elk or a soaring eagle.

Visit the Author Profile page at Harlequin.com.

FUGITIVE CHASE

JENNA NIGHT

LOVE INSPIRED SUSPENSE

INSPIRATIONAL ROMANCE

LOVE INSPIRED®SUSPENSE

INSPIRATIONAL ROMANCE

Recycling programs for this product may not exist in your area.

ISBN-13: 978-1-335-57464-0

Fugitive Chase

This edition published by arrangement with Harlequin Books S.A.

For questions and comments about the quality of this book, please contact us at CustomerService@Harlequin.com.

Love Inspired
22 Adelaide St. West, 40th Floor
Toronto, Ontario M5H 4E3, Canada
www.Harlequin.com

Printed in U.S.A.

For he shall give his angels charge over thee,
to keep thee in all thy ways.
–*Psalms* 91:11

To my mom, Esther.

ONE

"You can do this," Ramona Miller whispered to herself.

Loose gravel crunched beneath the soles of her shoes as she walked along the edge of a crumbling asphalt road. Her heart thudded heavily in her chest and fear squeezed her lungs so tightly she could barely take a breath.

On top of that, she was freezing. The night was dark with only a sliver of moon in the black sky. She would much rather be at home watching TV instead of walking alongside the marshy grass and tall pines just outside the city of Stone River in northern Idaho. But she was pretty sure she'd located the man she was searching for and she couldn't quit now. She just needed to get a glimpse of him and make certain he really was Darrin Linder, a fugitive from justice. Darrin had skipped his court date for charges related to drug dealing and assault. His bail bond had been revoked. He was a wanted man. And he had repeatedly threatened Ramona's family.

She continued past the weathered wooden sign announcing the Western Trails Resort. The resort was a collection of small cabins scattered among the trees on the backside of Lake Bell. In the summer, the place would be packed with vacationers, but right now, in the chilly off-season of early spring, she could see lights only in the office building and three of the cabins.

She knew which cabin she was interested in, but she also knew this could be another false lead.

She'd thought she'd found Darrin a couple of times before and called the cops, but she'd been mistaken. The police had shown up for nothing. She was pretty sure they'd decided that she was a kook.

This time she would make certain Darrin was here before she called them again.

She crossed the road, using the forest for cover. It was a quiet night and she tried not to make any noise. She'd parked her car a short distance away so she wouldn't draw anyone's attention as she made her approach.

The windows on the cabin had tired-looking blinds with gaps between several of the horizontal slats. She would get up close and take a quick peek inside—and just hope he didn't catch her in the act.

The drugs Darrin used and sold made him mean and paranoid—and extremely dangerous, far beyond what his limited criminal record would suggest. There were witnesses to Darrin's dangerous, illicit behavior who were too afraid to speak out against him to the authorities. Among them was Ramona's cousin, Jasmine, who also happened to be Darrin's former girlfriend.

Ramona's hand trembled as she patted her back jeans pocket to make sure her phone was still there. Then she continued her approach.

She just needed to get a glimpse of him or hear his voice. Then she'd call the police and report his location, all while hurrying back to the relative safety of her car.

Her mouth was dry as she moved closer. She crouched down, crept up to the window and listened. She heard voices, but nothing distinct enough to prove Darrin was in there. She peeked in and saw a man she didn't recognize. He was skinny, with long, stringy hair.

Disappointment mingled with relief. She hadn't seen Darrin, but at least the man who was inside the cabin hadn't seen her.

Then Darrin walked across her field of vision, looking like the handsome young professional that Jasmine had fallen in love with and that their family had welcomed with open arms. Not at all like the monster they now knew him to be.

She had him. *You're not going to hurt anybody else.*

She was elated, yet at the same time frightened to be this close to him. Her pulse pounded so hard in her ears that it drowned out nearly every other sound. For several long seconds she was frozen in fear and couldn't move even though she desperately wanted to.

Finally, she forced herself away from the window. She reached for her phone as she turned toward the forest to make her getaway.

An arm shot out toward her and a hand clamped tightly around her throat.

Ramona's mouth jerked open in surprise, but she couldn't draw enough air into her lungs to scream. Fear sent icy tremors shooting throughout her body.

She knew she had to do something, but she was too scared to think of anything.

Her attacker was a large man with a shaved head and tattoos of two wriggling snakes on the sides of his neck. From the little bit of light of spilling out of the window she could see his eyes. They had an oddly vacant look about them. He probably used the same drugs that Darrin did.

Desperation pushed past her fear and she clawed at the hand gripping her throat, frantically trying to peel away the man's thick fingers. When that didn't work, she punched and kicked at him. He seemed oblivious to the blows that landed on him, and a wide grin crawled across his face.

"What do we have here?" he asked, sounding delighted that he'd caught her.

A slow, spinning sensation had Ramona feeling as if she were about to pass out, and she clawed even more desperately at the man's hand. How could she have been so stupid? She *knew* the drugs Darrin used made him paranoid. She should have guessed that he'd post a lookout on the grounds outside the cabin.

In a lightning-quick move, the man let go of her throat and clamped his hand over her mouth. Then he grabbed her arm. "Let's get inside so you can say hi to the guys."

He dragged her around to the front door, opened it and pulled her in alongside him. "Found a snoop," he called out.

The skinny guy Ramona had seen through the window snatched a handgun from the tabletop beside him and pointed it at her.

Her body trembled uncontrollably as her gaze darted toward the other side of the cabin. She heard the scrape of a chair moving over the floor. And then Darrin stepped into view.

From a distance, he looked like he used to—thick blond hair styled and gelled into place, wearing a crisp long-sleeved, blue-pinstriped shirt and dark blue slacks.

Up close, he looked different. His eyes had the same emptiness as the bald guy who still held onto her. His face looked gaunt and was settled into an angry expression. The harsh, straight line of his mouth quirked upward at one corner as he took several swaggering steps toward her.

"She was looking in the window," the bald man said.

Darrin glanced toward several gray duffel bags that were zipped up and stacked on the floor in the main room of the cabin. What was in them? Drugs?

Finally, the bald man removed his hand from her mouth, but he kept hold of her arm.

"I didn't see anything," Ramona quickly spat out, hoping that would encourage them to let her go.

"Ramona," Darrin said calmly. "What a pleasant surprise." His gaze raked over her from head to toe and then came back up to her face. "You really do look remarkably like your cousin. Are you here to take Jasmine's former place in my life? I'm flattered."

What? He thought she wanted to be his new girlfriend? Disgust made her recoil from him, but she couldn't go far since the bald guy still held onto her.

"You know this woman?" Bald Guy asked.

Darrin nodded. "I know her whole family." He stepped closer toward her. "So, why are you really here? And how did you find me?"

"I just wanted to see if we could talk. Maybe settle the tension between you and my family." Her words sounded unbelievable, even to Ramona, but she was scared and she couldn't think of anything better to say.

"Let her go," he said to the bald guy.

The guy released her and Ramona quickly stepped away. Her lungs were still tight with fear, but she could breathe a little more easily now. And the added oxygen seemed to be prompting her brain cells to function normally again.

Obviously, she had to get out of here, *fast*. It looked as if she'd interrupted some kind of meeting. Which meant more bad guys could show up at any minute.

"You *know* I haven't seen anything," she said, her voice sounding shakier than she intended as she tried to reason with him. She lifted her hand and gestured around the room, ignoring the duffel bags. "There's nothing for me *to* see. So, I'll just get going."

She had her phone. All she needed to do was get outside so she could call the cops.

Darrin pursed his lips together and looked at her thoughtfully. "I figured I might see some fireworks from Jasmine after she decided to go to the police instead of staying loyal to me. She was always a little wild. It was one of the things I loved most about her." He smiled to himself. "But you were always the sensible one. Or so you seemed. I know you convinced Jasmine to leave me, to turn against me, but I never imagined you'd show up in person and cause me more trouble."

"No trouble," Ramona said, holding up both hands in a placating gesture. "I'll just go." She started to move toward the door, but Bald Guy blocked her path.

"What do I have to do to make you and your family shut up and mind your own business?" Darrin asked, sounding like a weary teacher addressing a problem student.

Without warning he snatched the front of her jacket and pulled her toward him. "Tell me how you found me."

"Let go of me!" She tried to pull free and they grappled for a few seconds until he slapped her, hard. She was stunned. Her cheek felt numb from the impact. And then it began to burn.

"I'm not playing," Darrin said in a low voice. "You, Jasmine and everybody else in your stupid family need to keep your mouths shut. Nobody talks to the cops. Nobody follows me again or you'll regret it. And I *will* get you to tell me exactly how you found me."

Jasmine was the one who had told Ramona where Darrin would be. She'd gotten the information through a friend of hers. If Darrin found out, he would kill Jasmine.

"Start loading everything into the cars," he ordered his companions. "We're going to have to move locations." He cut his gaze to Ramona, glaring at her through eyes dark with hatred. "You're lying. You saw the guns. You saw the drugs. You know what's going on and you want to turn me in to the cops."

Guns and drugs. So that was what was in the bags. She hadn't seen them—but his words made it clear that he wouldn't believe her protests. And now that he'd confirmed what was going on, there was no way he was going to let her go.

Behind her, Ramona could hear Darrin's two cohorts grabbing the duffel bags, opening the cabin door and heading outside.

Darrin finally let go of her jacket, only to reach into Ramona's back jeans pocket and pull out her phone. Her heavy heart sank even further. He must have felt it while she'd been struggling to break free from him. He glanced at the screen and then flung the phone against the wall. When it landed on the floor, she could see the cover was cracked and the screen had gone to solid blue.

He turned to her. "You're coming with us."

No. She was not going with them. She could guess how the night would end for her if she did.

Darrin stepped toward the dinette table in the alcove to reach for something she couldn't see.

Ramona had a split second to make a decision. She realized she had nothing to lose by trying to escape, so she ran.

Through the main room of the cabin, out the front door that had been left open by Darrin's accomplices and across the grass. She didn't look for the two thugs she knew were somewhere out there. She just kept her gaze focused straight ahead. *Dear Lord, help!*

Behind her she could hear Darrin, Bald Guy and Skinny Guy yelling to each other.

She headed for the cover of the forest, running between the tall pines, zigzagging as best she could. Her lungs were already burning so she pushed herself to keep going as fast as possible. She could still hear the men behind her. They seemed to have split up, fanning out to cast a wider net as they hunted for her.

Bounty hunter Harry Orlansky had just arrived at the Western Trails Resort. He'd cut the engine and was sitting in the darkened interior of his pickup truck ready to start conducting surveillance when a woman ran out the door of one of the cabins.

He'd already used his night-vision binoculars to check out the two men who'd come out a minute or two ahead of her and he'd determined that neither one was the bail jumper he was after. He hadn't been there for long and he was already wondering if the lead that had brought him here was going to pan out when he saw the woman dart out of the cabin.

His target, Darrin Linder, was hot on her heels. And it looked like Linder had a gun. The other two men who'd been outside the cabin pulled pistols from their waistbands and also started chasing after the woman.

Harry's heartbeat sped up and adrenaline flooded his body. That woman was fleeing for her life. He had to help her.

He fired up the truck's engine and pulled onto the narrow road, heading roughly parallel to the route he'd seen the woman running.

Harry knew this area well, and if the woman continued running in the same general direction, she'd eventually intersect with the curving highway that wrapped around the lake. He would speed down the road until he was certain he was ahead of her, then he'd get out of the truck and start working his way back through the forest toward her on foot.

As he shot down the road, it occurred to him that he recognized the woman from somewhere. But before he could worry about identifying her, he needed to report back to the rest of his team.

Harry was alone on this hunt since the rest of the team was following up on another, more dangerous felon. Linder faced drug and assault charges, but neither charge involved use of a deadly weapon, so when the tip came in regarding his whereabouts, the team had decided that Harry could capture Linder alone while everybody else went after the felon. Harry's instructions were to check in with them at regular intervals and to call for backup if needed.

Harry made a call to his boss, Cassie Wheeler—the owner of Rock Solid Bail Bonds. She answered on the first ring. "Hey, Harry. What have you got?"

He quickly described the situation.

"Sounds to me like I better call the cops and have them head your way," Cassie responded calmly.

"Agreed." He steered the truck to the side of the road and stopped.

"Do you need anything else from me? Need me to stay on the line?"

"Nope."

"Don't get yourself shot," she said before disconnecting.

"I'll do my best," Harry muttered to himself as he slid out of the truck. He strapped on a bulletproof vest over his shirt and holstered his pistol. He already had pepper spray and cuffs on his belt. He grabbed the night-vision binoculars.

He crossed the tree line into the forest,

positioning himself at his best guess of where the woman might emerge.

About twenty yards in, he stopped to listen. At first, he didn't hear anything other than the normal sounds of a forest at nighttime. Then he heard the squeak of branches shifting. It might just be the wind. Or it could be someone moving through the woods.

Harry had not survived two tours in Afghanistan and nearly three years as a bounty hunter by assuming the best-case scenario. Better safe than sorry. Right now, he assumed the sounds he heard came from a person or persons. For his own safety, he needed to prepare for the idea that it was Linder or one of the other two armed goons rather than the woman.

A sound like a small rockslide caught his attention. Someone was headed downhill in his direction, dislodging dirt and rocks along the way. He crouched down and waited. A few seconds later he heard more sounds of someone crashing through the woods. Then, looking through the night-vision binoculars, he saw her. The woman who'd run out of the cabin.

He heard more footsteps and the sound of more branches snapping just a short distance away. And then more rocks and loosened dirt began to slide down the sloping ground. The men who were chasing her were closing in. Harry saw one of them, but where were the other two?

Staying crouched, he moved to a spot where he could sit with his back pressed up against a tree. Then he cautiously stood up and took another look around. The woman was still moving forward, but not very quickly, her pace more like a jog. She was obviously getting tired, but she was almost to the spot where Harry silently waited for her. Unfortunately, they were not in a situation where he could politely walk up and introduce himself to her. With the bad guys so close on her heels, he was forced to sprint over and tackle her.

Somebody in the forest opened fire just as Harry knocked the woman to the ground. The shots came from one direction, indicating a single shooter. The blasts tore bark off of tree trunks and sent jagged splinters of wood flying all around them.

Harry shielded the woman's body with his own, though she wasn't making it easy for him. She squirmed and kicked and flailed, trying to push him off of her. He had her head tucked beneath his chest and he moved just a little so he could tell her, "I'm not one of them. I'm trying to help you."

She kept flailing a little longer, but she finally stopped. He couldn't tell if she believed him or if she was just worn out.

The shooting stopped. Harry heard a man's voice saying, "What's going on? Did you find her? Is it done?" The voice sounded tinny. Harry realized it was coming through the speaker on a walkie-talkie or a phone. That must be how the three pursuers were coordinating their chase.

"I don't know if I got her or not." This voice was not transmitted over a line. It was someone standing close to them. Presumably the shooter. "Start moving in my direction."

"Is that Darrin Linder's voice?" Harry whispered. "Is he the one who was shooting at us?"

Eyes wide with fear, the woman nodded.

Harry could hear the other two men tromping through the forest toward them. Harry looked down at the woman. They couldn't stay here. They'd be found.

He gestured at her to stay quiet, then he got up and helped her rise into a squat beside him. He pressed his phone and truck keys into her hand. Then he leaned toward her, his breath stirring her hair as he spoke close to her ear. "My truck is parked on the road." He pointed in the direction where he'd left it. "Run for it and drive out of here as fast as you can. The cops are already on their way, but call 9-1-1 anyway and tell them shots were fired."

"What about you?" she asked.

"I'll lead them in the other direction."

She hesitated, so he gave her a little push. But before either of them could get moving, Harry heard the sound of several vehicles pulling up to a stop on the highway. Then he heard the sounds of communication over a police radio. Flashes of bright white from a high-power flashlight flickered through the trees.

"Cops!" one of the men in the forest yelled.

"This isn't over, Ramona!" Darrin Linder called out. "You better make sure you keep your mouth shut! If you don't, I'll find you. I'll silence you and your whole family. *For good!*"

TWO

"So, you really *aren't* Darrin Linder's girlfriend?" the bounty hunter asked Ramona. They were standing outside the cabin Darrin and his cohorts had used. Inside, a police investigation was now underway.

"From the moment I first saw you, I thought you looked familiar," he continued. He tilted his head and lifted his chin, looking down at her like didn't quite believe her. "You look a lot like Jasmine Castillo."

Tired of being intimidated, Ramona met his suspicious gaze and held it.

In the illumination from the porch light, she could see that the man who'd saved her life had dark blue eyes. She hadn't been able to see what color they were in the darkness of the forest, but she had noticed that he was a big guy with a lot of muscle when he tackled her.

Although she was aggravated with the suspicious look he was giving her, she had to admit she felt a tug of attraction to him. That could be due to the kindness he'd shown her despite his rough appearance, hinting at a personality with character and depth to it. Or perhaps it was the simple appeal of a man who'd been willing to risk his own life to save hers. He'd made her feel protected when she needed it most.

Stop. She would not let her thoughts travel any further down that path.

After a recent bout with pneumonia and a lengthy recovery, she'd taken inventory of her life, set some goals and made herself some promises. One of those promises was that she would try for a committed relationship—a genuine, lasting love. No more wasting her time with fixer-upper boyfriends or men who carried too much emotional baggage. She had a history with that kind of thing and had finally realized she was choosing relationships with lots of drama because they kept the focus on her partner and she never had to truly open her heart or be vulnerable.

Her recent heath scare had reminded her that life was fleeting. She hoped to get married someday. She wanted a family. She'd decided she was finished playing games and she was ready to woman up and take her chances with a real, honest relationship. One with a future.

The man standing in front of her was a *bounty hunter*. He no doubt lived on drama and chaos. The new Ramona, the one who was looking for a sane and stable relationship, was not going to allow herself be attracted to him. No, thank you.

Forcing herself to look away from him, she glanced into the cabin where a pair of crime scene technicians were processing the area, searching for evidence. With them on the porch stood Sergeant Gabe Bergman, the officer who had taken Ramona's statement while the bounty hunter and several officers searched the woods and the road for Linder and his partners. Unfortunately, as she'd learned when the bounty hunter had returned, the criminals had vanished.

"I know I look like Jasmine," she said wearily. She was tired of the questioning and the suspicion, but she was also just plain tired. And her lungs hurt. She was learning that it takes quite a while to completely heal from pneumonia. "Jasmine is my cousin," she continued. "And she isn't Darrin's girlfriend. Not anymore. She broke up with him a month ago. My name is Ramona Miller."

The bounty hunter glanced at Sergeant Bergman.

"She's telling you the truth," the sergeant responded. He'd seen her identification when she'd given her statement describing what had happened. One of the crime scene techs stepped out of the cabin, beckoned to the sergeant, and Bergman walked over to talk to her, leaving Ramona and the bounty hunter alone.

"So, who exactly are you?" she asked him.

"Harry Orlansky. My boss put up the bond that got Darrin Linder out of jail. He skipped his court date, so I was planning on dragging him back to lockup. Now that he's fired shots at us, I am that much more motivated to catch him and throw him back behind bars where he belongs."

Feeling a flush of irritation, Ramona crossed her arms over her chest. "He should never have been let out to begin with."

"A judge thought otherwise," Harry said evenly. "I tried to contact your cousin and get her to help me find Linder. She ignored my voice mails and text messages. They might not be as broken up as you think they are. I believe she's protecting him."

"I doubt that very much." Ramona took a deep breath and blew it out, trying to push away the heavy weight of frustration and despair that settled on her shoulders whenever she thought about her cousin.

Jasmine had a heart of gold, but she also had emotional issues after her dad fled town with another woman, abandoning her and her mom back when Jasmine was just twelve. She didn't always make good decisions, and she didn't handle stress very well. Getting messages from a bounty hunter had probably freaked her out, even though she did want Darrin caught and locked up. Unfortunately, it had become her habit to ignore a problem and hope it somehow fixed itself.

A police officer walked toward them from the resort's office building with a young man alongside him. Sergeant Bergman stepped forward and the two lawmen met near where Harry and Ramona were standing.

"The desk clerk has some information on the man who rented the cabin," the officer said.

Ramona felt a spark of hope. Maybe Darrin was about to get caught.

The clerk described Darrin's skinny, stringy-haired cohort as the renter. He'd registered under the name Albert Mason, saying he would be the only guest and that he would be staying for a single night. He'd registered one vehicle.

The resort required a credit card number to book a stay in case there were damages to the cabin, but the man only had cash. The clerk had made a quick call to the property owner and an agreement was reached for a nonrefundable damage deposit of a hundred dollars, paid up front, with the proviso that "Albert" agreed to let the clerk inspect the cabin for damages before he checked out tomorrow morning.

Using the computer in his unmarked

patrol car, Sergeant Bergman quickly determined that the home address, driver's license information, cell phone number and license plate number Albert gave the clerk were all fake.

Security in the resort's office was nearly nonexistent, with only one low-quality video camera in the lobby and no cameras outside the building. The officer who interviewed the clerk already had the evening's security footage downloaded onto his tablet. He played the segment of video that covered the time span of when Albert was in the office. There was no clear image of Albert's face.

"Weak security is probably the reason they chose this property instead of a hotel," Harry said.

"But why would they need to rent a cabin at all?" Ramona asked. She turned to Sergeant Bergman. "Those duffel bags I told you about were filled with drugs and guns. Darrin admitted as much. I think that Darrin and the other two men were here to meet someone—maybe a buyer. But why not do that out in the woods where nobody could see them?"

"It would be too easy for either one of the parties to set up an ambush," the sergeant answered. "A shooter could hide in the shadows, kill everybody on the opposite side of the transaction and then leave with everything—the money and the goods. Happens all the time with drug deals. Places like these cabins or hotel rooms allow for privacy but still have the protection of enclosed spaces and potential witnesses if things get out of hand. They encourage all the players to keep their behavior under control."

Ramona shook her head. "I can't imagine living that kind of life." It was unnerving to think of Darrin that way when he'd nearly been part of their family. Darrin had been invited to family gatherings. He'd shared family meals with Ramona, her parents and Jasmine's mom, Valerie. And then he'd turned on them.

Fear, cold and clammy, slithered in the pit of her stomach. She shivered and rubbed her hands over her arms. Great, now she was cold inside and out.

"You all right?" the sergeant asked. "I can take you to the hospital to get checked out."

"No, thank you, I'm fine." Physically, Ramona was all right. Emotionally, she was starting to unravel.

Sergeant Bergman got a call over his radio. "Be careful," he said to Ramona before he walked toward his car to take the call.

The clerk was already headed back toward his office. The cop who'd interviewed him walked toward the cabin where the crime scene techs were still at work.

Ramona was left standing alone with the bounty hunter. She exhaled and watched the small cloud of vapor drift away on the cold night air, wondering if she should tell her parents what had happened or if she should keep it to herself so they wouldn't worry.

"I'll drive you home," Harry said.

"My car is parked down the road a short distance away. I'll be fine."

"You've been through a lot—you probably shouldn't be driving. I'll bring you back to get your car tomorrow morning."

His stubborn insistence was annoying. But if it hadn't been for him, Darrin would have caught up with her in the forest. He probably would have shot and killed her.

"Thank you for saving my life," she said.

He shrugged. "Mostly I was just focused on saving myself."

That wasn't true. And that hint of self-deprecating humor behind the man's obvious strength and capability made her curious about him.

"Before I take you home, would you be willing to go back to the bail bond office with me?" Harry asked. "You could meet some of the people I work with and help us come up with ideas on how to find Linder."

"The police are already doing everything possible to find him."

"Yes." Harry nodded. "They have their way of hunting for somebody and I have mine. Both ways can work, but if I find him first, I get paid."

Well, he certainly had motive for finding Darrin as quickly as possible. And wasn't that what she wanted?

A rustling sound in the forest startled her. After a moment, she realized it was just the breeze rustling the tree branches. Still, for a few seconds her heart raced at the thought that it might be Darrin. He'd issued threats before, but now he seemed focused on coming after her and her family.

"Okay," she said to Harry. "I'll go with you. I'll do everything I can to help put Darrin Linder behind bars where he belongs."

* * *

"We won't stop looking for Linder until he's in custody," Cassie Wheeler, the owner of Rock Solid Bail Bonds, assured Ramona. The bondswoman cast a glance at Harry. "For one thing, he fired shots at my bounty hunter. He could have killed him. Do you have any idea how tedious and time-consuming it is to hire and train a new bounty hunter?"

Harry lifted an eyebrow. "It's good to be appreciated."

Joking aside, he knew that Cassie truly cared about her employees. She'd grown up in the business, inheriting it from her father, and she treated her employees like family. If she hadn't been in the middle of coordinating the recovery of another felon when Harry called tonight, Cassie probably would have shown up on the scene ahead of the cops.

Cassie tucked her straight, strawberry blond hair behind her ears. That was typically a sign that she was getting serious.

"You sure you're all right?" Cassie asked Ramona, putting her hands on her hips and wearing the expression that Harry thought of as her interrogation look. "Because you don't look like you're all right."

"I think the reality of nearly getting killed tonight is sinking in," Ramona said. "But I want to be here. I want to help put a stop to Darrin's drug dealing and violence. I want to keep my family safe."

Ramona was obviously a strong woman. Harry had always been attracted to strong women. A familiar ache began to blossom in his chest as his thoughts turned toward his late wife, Willa. She'd been gone three years now. Some days it felt like thirty years. Other days, it felt like he'd been talking with her just a few hours ago.

He let his gaze travel back to Ramona.

Willa had been tall, blond, blue-eyed and freckled. Ramona was average height, with dark hair and hazel eyes. But there was something achingly familiar in the way she straightened her shoulders and set her chin as she stated her commitment to protecting her family.

Harry brushed the thought aside. It didn't matter what Ramona looked like or what kind of character she had. So what if she was the most interesting woman Harry had met in a long time? He was not looking to replace Willa. His late wife deserved better. She had been unfailingly faithful and supportive during the four short years of their marriage, even though much of that time had been while he was deployed overseas.

Willa had been loyal to him. How could he not remain loyal to her?

"We appreciate your willingness to help us," Cassie said to Ramona. "You've met Harry, obviously. The gentleman standing in the doorway is Leon Bragg."

Ramona looked over at the big guy, a little older than Harry, who stood at the front of the hallway that led to a couple of smaller offices and a breakroom. "Nice to meet you," Leon said politely.

"We have another bounty hunter who works out of this office. His name is Martin Silverdeer, but he isn't here right now," Cassie added.

"Where *is* Martin?" Harry directed his question to Leon.

"Getting the offender we captured earlier this evening checked in at county lockup." He threw Harry a triumphant half smile filled with the promise of a detailed description of how the arrest went down sometime later.

They'd all been standing, but now Cassie moved toward a mahogany-colored leather sofa and matching easy chairs. "Let's sit."

Harry appreciated Cassie's willingness to invest in decent furniture for the office. It was nice for a man his size to be able to drop down onto a chair and not have to worry about breaking it. The office had a Western look with bold colors, pine desks and tables, and calming paintings of local rivers and mountains hanging on the walls. On especially rough days, the homey feel made the job a little bit easier.

Ramona sat on the couch. Harry sat in a nearby easy chair.

"Would you like a cup of coffee?" Cassie asked Ramona.

Some people in Cassie's position—anxious to recover a fugitive so she wouldn't lose her bond money—might be tempted to immediately press Ramona for information. But Cassie's instincts were good and she knew they'd likely get more useful information from Ramona if they all stayed calm and took things slow.

Ramona nodded. "Coffee sounds good."

"I'll get some started," Leon offered, then turned and disappeared down the hallway. A few seconds later Harry could hear water running in the office's small kitchen.

Ramona sank back into the sofa, sighed

deeply and then reached up to run her hands through her hair. She looked startled as she plucked a few pine needles free. Her gaze dropped to her lap, and when she looked up, tears had collected in the corners of her eyes. She blinked, and they began to roll down her cheeks.

"Hey, you're okay," Harry said, leaning toward her and nearly placing his hands atop hers. But then he caught himself. She didn't know him and what he intended as a reassuring gesture might make her feel uncomfortable.

"You're safe here," he said, leaning back.

Cassie grabbed a box of tissues from a desk, handed it to Ramona and then sat down beside her, making small talk as Ramona dabbed at her eyes.

A few minutes later Leon appeared with a coffeepot and some cups. Ramona took hers with sugar and a splash of cream, like Harry did. After a couple of sips, she started to breathe more calmly and the pinched expression on her face relaxed a little.

"How can I help you find Darrin?" she eventually asked. "The cops are finally out actively looking for him. At least that's one thing I accomplished tonight. What makes you think you can find him if they can't?"

"The police have access to technology, personnel and a mountain of data that we don't have," Cassie explained. "On the other hand, there are people who are afraid of cops or don't like them. They won't talk to the police but they will talk to us. And sometimes we just happen upon information that the authorities don't have."

Ramona nodded. "That makes sense."

"Do you have any idea where Darrin Linder might be?" Harry asked. "Any thoughts on where he might hide out? Can you tell us who his friends are, where he likes to hang out, things like that?"

She shook her head. "No. I wasn't exactly friends with him. But Jasmine would know."

"You really do look like her," Cassie interjected while looking at a photo of Jasmine on a tablet. "No wonder Harry thought you were her at first." She shifted her gaze to Ramona. "How did your cousin get tied up with a jerk like Darrin Linder?"

Ramona closed her eyes and drew in a deep breath. When she opened her eyes and spoke, her voice was steady.

"They were introduced to each other by someone Jasmine worked with. I was living with Jasmine at the time, so I was around him a little bit at the beginning of their relationship. He seemed like a nice enough guy. He had a job selling heavy equipment to farms and ranches all over the state. He made good money.

"And then I had issues with a personal situation and had to move back in with my parents."

Ramona's use of the word *situation*

jumped out at Harry like a verbal red flag. What kind of situation was she talking about? Did it have anything to do with Darrin Linder? But he didn't ask her any of the many questions popping into his mind right now. He didn't want her to get defensive and withdraw her cooperation.

"Very quickly, Darrin moved in with Jasmine," Ramona continued. "I didn't see much of her for a while. About three months later, when I finally did see her, things had changed." She paused and shook her head. "Jasmine had trouble with depression for years, but she didn't want to get professional help with it. And that made her vulnerable to a predator like Darrin."

While listening to her story, Harry saw events from his own life in his mind's eye. He'd battled depression after finishing each of his combat tours overseas. The struggle was compounded by grief and sorrow after Willa passed away. His faith had saved him, but even so, it had been a tough experience and he was glad he'd taken his dad's suggestion and seen a counselor.

"Darrin had some friend who'd gotten him started on drugs, telling him they'd give him an edge in his job," Ramona said in a flat tone, like she was trying to separate her emotions from the words she was saying. "They were supposed to help him make more sales, earn more money, get more done every day. And they seemed to work, making him feel more energetic and happier. And he convinced Jasmine that those drugs could help her, too.

"For a while, they did make her feel better. And then they began to make her feel worse. But by then she couldn't stop taking them. Meanwhile, Darrin had turned into a different person. He became aggressive and paranoid. He slapped Jasmine on several different occasions, but she refused to call the police. She refused to deal with the situation.

"A little over a month ago, she hit bottom and finally opened up to me. She told me Darrin had started selling drugs and that he was earning so much money doing it that he quit his regular job. I finally got her to see a doctor and get help for her addiction. She went to church with me for the first time in a long while. She broke things off with Darrin and told him to move out. He slapped her again, hard enough to knock her to the ground, and this time she called the police and pressed charges. He was furious. He blamed our family for turning Jasmine against him.

"Finally, he got caught selling drugs and was arrested. We were relieved until he got out on bail. He started stalking and harassing Jasmine. Told her he still loved her—but when she told him to leave, he switched to threatening her. Then he threatened my Aunt Valerie, and then my parents, and then me."

Her voice trembled and more tears broke free. Cassie handed her another tissue. Harry found himself impatiently tapping the heels of his boots on the floor, anxious to get out of the office and go hunting for the pathetic jerk who'd made the lives of Ramona and her family so miserable.

Cassie gave Harry a pointed look. He realized what he was doing and stopped tapping.

"Jasmine heard that he might be at the resort tonight. I figured out he was in that particular cabin because the cars parked outside the other cabins had out-of-state plates. I didn't intend to confront Darrin," Ramona said softly. "I just wanted to verify that he was there before I called the police."

"Sounds like we want to talk to the person who told Jasmine where to find Linder," Leon said.

Harry nodded in agreement.

"How did *you* find Darrin?" Ramona asked Harry.

"A paid informant saw a guy he thought might be Linder but he wasn't sure. He followed him out to the resort and then called me. I'd just gotten there, hadn't even had time to take pictures of the cars parked in front of the cabin, when I saw you running out the cabin door."

"Thank You, Lord, for putting someone there to help me," Ramona said, hugging herself.

"Amen," Harry said. Cassie and Leon nodded in agreement.

"Would you be willing to take me to talk to Jasmine?" Harry asked. "Tonight, if possible. She's our best hope for solid information that could help us find Linder."

"I can do that." Ramona reached toward the back pocket on her jeans and then suddenly stopped, dropping her hand back into her lap. "Darrin broke my phone."

"Use mine," Harry said.

Ramona tapped a number on the screen. The call apparently went to voice mail and she left a message. "I knew she wouldn't answer because she wouldn't recognize the number," she said after disconnecting. And then her eyes widened as a look of alarm crossed her face.

She got to her feet. "Let's drive over to her condo right now." She drew in a shaky breath. "Darrin was furious. You saw that. You heard him threaten my family. I hope he hasn't gone after Jasmine."

THREE

Harry drove while Ramona gave him directions to Jasmine's home, finally telling him to take a right turn onto a short street with a row of eight condos on one side. They were nice, new, two-story buildings conveniently located within walking distance of downtown.

Harry had grown up on the outskirts of Stone River and he remembered when this stretch of land housed an old sawmill. Back when he was a kid, after the sawmill closed and the local economy tanked, he'd overheard his parents and grandparents fretting about young people moving away and the town dying out. But in the years since then, thanks to aggressive action by the city planners and city council, it had become a prime destination for retirees, outdoor enthusiasts and people who wanted a second home on the edge of the wilderness.

Ramona directed him to the third condo from the end. Harry pulled to the curb on the opposite side of the street and parked. Immediately, she reached for her door handle. Harry quickly stuck out his arm to keep her from getting out of the truck.

"What?" she asked sharply, turning to face him.

In the faint light from a streetlight, he could see the anxiety etched on her face. She wanted to race inside and check on her cousin.

"Just a precaution," he said coolly. He shifted his gaze to the rearview mirror. "I want to make sure we're not walking into a trap." Harry wasn't taking any chances. He'd considered having Leon come with them, but then decided that he didn't want to draw too much attention to this visit. Especially if it might make Jasmine nervous. And Leon was just a call away if Harry needed him.

The condos were the only structures currently on the street, though half of the block opposite the condos had been graded and leveled. A few tagged stakes were poking out of the ground, presumably marking future floor plans. There was no reason for there to be much traffic through here.

Harry made sure they sat there for a full five minutes. Beside him, Ramona began to nervously chew on her bottom lip.

There were no sounds of distress coming from inside the condo and nothing looked amiss. He had no indication that Jasmine was in imminent danger or needed his help. And right now, his priority was keeping Ramona safe.

Again, unbidden, his thoughts turned back to Willa. He hadn't been able to protect her from the death that had come so suddenly and unexpectedly. There'd been nothing he could do to save her. Accepting the fact that there were situations he couldn't control, battles he wouldn't win, and people that he couldn't rescue was a struggle that he faced every single day. And if it weren't for his faith, he would have lost that struggle a long time ago.

As soon as he was reasonably certain they wouldn't be walking into danger, he reached for his door handle. "Let's go."

The large window on the first floor of Jasmine's condo showed a little bit of light around the edges of the blinds. The rest of the windows were dark. The attached garage door was shut and it was hard to tell if anybody was home.

Harry looked around for video cameras as they approached the front door but he couldn't see any. "What kind of home security does she have?"

"She's got decent locks on the doors and windows," Ramona answered. "But that's it."

Harry knocked on the door.

"Jasmine!" Ramona called out. "Are you okay?"

The porch light flicked on and Harry stepped forward, putting himself between Ramona and the door just in case Linder was inside the condo with Jasmine.

"Who is it?" a female voice called out. "Who's there?"

"It's me!" Ramona hollered from behind Harry. "Are you okay? Open the door!"

The wooden door swung open and Harry found himself facing a woman who looked a lot like Ramona. But her eyes were a little rounder than Ramona's, her lips were thinner and her hair was a little bit shorter.

Harry looked past her shoulder to see if there was anyone else with her. The living room was empty. Farther back he could see a family room where the TV was on. "Is anyone else here?" he asked.

Jasmine stared wordlessly at him in response, obviously wondering who he was and what was happening.

Ramona darted around him and grabbed her cousin in an embrace, exclaiming, "I'm so glad you're all right."

"What's going on?" Jasmine endured the hug for several seconds before gently prying herself free from Ramona. "I got your message from a strange number saying you wanted to come by. I called you back at your number, but you didn't answer and I didn't know what to think." She stepped backward into her home as Ramona and Harry stepped forward.

"So, *is* anyone else here?" Ramona asked.

Jasmine shook her head. "No, it's just me. Why? What's going on?"

Harry closed the door behind them and engaged the locks.

Ramona introduced Harry to Jasmine. Then, as Ramona told her cousin about everything that had happened to her tonight, Harry tried to listen for the sounds of anyone walking around upstairs. He didn't know Jasmine, so he couldn't afford to believe what she said without question. Linder could be up there and she could be hiding him for some reason.

Jasmine burst into tears when Ramona finished her story. "I'm so sorry that happened to you. You could have been *killed*." She shook her head. "It's all my fault."

"No, it's not," Ramona said firmly. "Darrin is responsible for his own behavior."

"But I'm the one who let him into my life," she said in a wavering voice. "I introduced him to our family."

"Have you seen Darrin at all today?" Harry interjected, intent on keeping everyone on task. The task being to find Darrin Linder—plus his two cronies, if possible—and lock them up.

Jasmine used the backs of her hands to wipe the tears from her eyes. "No. I haven't seen him today. But he still finds ways to bump into me at the coffee shop or one of the restaurants near my work, even though I told him to stay away from me."

"Do you mind if I take a look around?" Harry asked. She sounded sincere—but that didn't mean she was telling the truth. Maybe she'd actually decided she loved Linder after all and she was hiding him. Stranger things had happened. Or maybe Darrin had shown up and threatened to hurt her if she told anyone he was here.

"You think I'm lying?" A stubborn expression crossed Jasmine's face and she crossed her arms over her chest.

"Just let him look," Ramona said.

"Oh, all right."

Harry searched both floors of the condo and didn't find anybody. When he came downstairs, both women were sitting on stools at the kitchen counter. Harry asked Jasmine if she had any idea where Darrin might be.

"I don't know where he moved to after

I finally kicked him out," she said. "Obviously he didn't go far since I still see him around town."

"What about his family?" Fugitives often looked to family for help. "Where do his parents live?"

"As far as I know, his entire family lives over around Seattle and Tacoma."

Harry worked his way through the standard list of questions. Within a half hour he had the names of Darrin's employer and a few friends Jasmine had met, plus the name of the person who'd told Jasmine that Darrin might be at the cabins tonight. It was a decent start. And while he wanted to keep pursuing Linder, it was already late in the evening. He wasn't a cop and couldn't pound on people's doors and demand they answer his questions without alienating them, so he would wait until a more suitable time tomorrow morning to question them.

"You might consider getting some decent security installed," he said to Jasmine. "Video cameras. Maybe a security monitoring company."

"Sounds expensive." She turned to Ramona. "But then, I've already had a few things repaired around here because they weren't done correctly in the first place. Maybe I can get Alex to install something at cost. The repairs were covered by the warranty that came with buying the place, but still, I think he owes me some kind of compensation for all the inconvenience it's caused."

"Alex is the builder of these condos," Ramona explained to Harry before turning back to Jasmine. "Getting this place more secure might take a while. Why don't you come home with me? My parents would love it. Or we could take you to your mom's house. I just don't think you should stay here alone. Darrin was dangerous before, but he's *really* dangerous now. And I'm afraid he'll come after you."

Jasmine sighed heavily and fixed her

gaze on Ramona. "You're probably in more danger from him than I am. You're a witness to the drugs and guns in his cabin. And he actually fired a gun at you and tried to *kill* you. If he gets captured, he'll have to face new charges for all of that—which means he'd go to prison for a long time."

Harry's concern for Ramona's safety ratcheted up a couple of notches because there was no doubt in his mind that Jasmine was right.

"I know how Darrin thinks," Jasmine continued. "He's not going to take responsibility for his actions tonight. He's going to blame you."

"It sounds like he blames all of us," Ramona said softly.

"I'll help you get your car back tomorrow," Harry said to Ramona when the two of them walked out of the condo a short time later. Right now, he just wanted to get her home as quickly as possible. He needed to know she would be safe. And, honestly, he wouldn't mind being around her for a few more minutes. Her fighting attitude and the tired smile she managed now and then despite all she'd been through tonight touched him.

He would sort out his feelings about that later. Right now, he just wanted to stay close and make sure she got home safely.

"Okay, thanks."

She gave him directions to the house where she lived with her parents, but was otherwise quiet. When they arrived, he got out of the truck and walked her to the door despite her protests that he didn't need to.

"You should stay home after we get your car tomorrow morning," Harry said as Ramona dug her house key out of her purse. "Lie low and give us a chance to find Linder."

"I've actually considered doing that. But my parents own and run a diner. We can't all stay home and I don't want to stay here by myself. I think going into work and being around other people might be the safest plan for me."

Harry wasn't crazy about the idea, but her reasoning made sense and he couldn't think of a better alternative. "Make certain you stay aware of your surroundings," he said.

"I will."

She unlocked the front door and stepped inside.

"Keep an eye out for Linder's two thugs," Harry added. "They could come after you, too."

Ramona sighed wearily. "I will. And thank you. For everything. Good night." She stepped inside and closed the door behind her.

Harry listened for the locks to engage and then walked back to his truck, determined to get this case wrapped up as quickly as possible. Linder and his cronies could not be left free to roam the streets of Stone River. They were too dangerous.

Police visited Jasmine at work this morning and questioned her about Darrin. Nobody's seen him. They think he probably left town right after the shooting. Might have left the state. Do you have any new leads?

Ramona tapped the screen on her new phone and sent the message to Harry.

Her phone chimed almost immediately with his reply.

Talking to one of the tenants in the apartment that Darrin claimed was his when he filled out his bond application. Visited his most recent place of employment earlier this morning.

Her phone chimed again before she could reply.

Watch your back. Police could be wrong. Linder or the other two guys could still be in town.

A familiar ripple of anxiety passed through her. She'd felt the same thing last night as she lay awake. After she'd told her parents about what had happened and reassured them that she was fine, she'd tossed and turned as fear and anger each took their turn sending dark, unsettling thoughts into her mind. She'd prayed all night, and it helped, but it was still a struggle that continued up until morning.

And it looked like it was going to continue throughout the day today, too. "Dear Lord, please protect my family and everyone searching for Darrin," she whispered softly. "Please help them find him and bring him to justice. And please give us Your peace that passes all understanding."

Another message came through on her phone.

I have some questions for you and Jasmine. What time will you be home from work?

She was supposed to work until two this afternoon, so she tapped in Two-thirty and hit Send. That would give her time to get home and change into clothes that didn't smell like pancake syrup and french fries. She didn't mind the smell, but some people did. That was the only reason for changing. It had nothing to do with wanting Harry to see her looking nicer. He'd already seen her in her work clothes, anyway, when he'd taken her to get her car this morning.

Ramona's parents could have helped her retrieve her car, but Harry had insisted on doing it because he'd promised her he would. He politely shook hands with her dad and let her mom hug him when they wanted to thank him for saving Ramona's life.

He'd also brought her the pay-as-you-go phone that she was using now so they could stay in touch while she was waiting to get her usual phone replaced. As the morning wore on, he'd texted her a couple of times with questions and updates. He seemed to be going out of his way for her, and she didn't know how to read the situation.

Yes, she did. The correct reading of the situation was that Harry was a decent man simply doing his job and Ramona was a slightly lonely woman who overthought things and desperately needed to put more effort into getting herself a romantic life.

Maybe she would actually do that once she was certain she and her family weren't going to be murdered by an enraged drug dealer who held them responsible for the dissolution of his love life.

"Would you start a fresh pot of decaf, honey? The stuff in the pot right now has been there for nearly an hour." Ramona's mom, Toni, smiled at her and gave her shoulder a playful nudge as she walked by. Her mom was trying to act like everything was fine, especially in front of the customers, but the dark circles under her eyes made it clear Toni hadn't slept much last night, either.

They were both behind the counter at her parents' diner, Kitchen Table, in downtown Stone River. They specialized in comfort food and right now they were just finishing up the lunch rush, which meant they'd been serving a lot of pot roast with mashed potatoes and meatloaf sandwiches on grilled sourdough.

"Sure, I'll take care of the coffee." Ramona smiled at her mom, going along with the pretense that everything was okay. It actually helped Ramona hold herself together. And she needed that. Because when her thoughts drifted back to what happened last night, fear squeezed her heart and for a moment it was like she was back in the woods outside the cabin, fighting for another breath as she ran for her life.

Normally, Ramona's parents came into the diner well before the sun was up and Ramona came in around midday and stayed until closing. Today had not been a normal day. Thanks to their loyal employees pitching in, her parents had been able to go in to work a little later this morning. And since Ramona hadn't wanted to stay home alone, and she definitely didn't want to be going home after dark, she'd come in earlier than usual with the intention of leaving in the afternoon.

Fortunately, the employees and regular customers who'd heard about the shooting and chase last night had managed to convey their concern for Ramona without being overly dramatic or asking for details. And that made it a little easier to get through her shift.

Ramona started the decaf brewing and then plated the two slices of Mile High Coconut Cream Pie she'd gone behind the counter to fetch from a cooler. She delivered the luscious dessert to the guests in a booth by the front window and smiled to herself at the look of wide-eyed delight on their faces.

And then her gaze shifted and she was looking out the window, her smile fading as anxiety kicked in again. She'd spent more time than usual today looking outside. She kept trying to remember what the two cars parked outside the cabin last night had looked like. She wished she'd paid more attention to them.

Did she really think she might see Darrin or his two accomplices driving by? The chances of that were pretty slim. Especially since the diner was only a couple of blocks from the police station.

"Excuse me. Are you okay?" The woman at the booth looked at Ramona with a deep frown crease between her silver eyebrows. She and her husband were traveling through north Idaho in their motor home. This was their first visit to the diner and they'd assured her it wouldn't be their last. Apparently, the poor woman had been trying to get Ramona's attention while Ramona stood right by her table, lost in thought.

She and her husband wanted carryout containers for their pie, explaining that they realized they couldn't finish it right now even though they wanted to. Ramona apologized profusely and hurried to the kitchen get the containers. How embarrassing. One minute she was so nervous and vigilant she was nearly jumping out of her skin. The next, she was lost in her thoughts and oblivious to someone speaking directly to her.

She hadn't had this problem before she'd been shot at. Hopefully the condition wouldn't last forever.

But it might. What if the police and bounty hunters never found Darrin? What if she had to go the rest of her life looking over her shoulder, wondering if he was closing in on her?

"Hey, Peanut," her dad called out to her as she passed by him in the kitchen. She'd come to terms with the fact that he was going to continue to use her childhood nickname no matter how old she got. "How ya holding up?" he asked.

"I'm okay, Dad."

Eric Miller was a tall, slender man who loved to feed people. He'd learned his trade in the US Navy where he'd observed the power that comfort food had to bring people together and help them smile or de-stress a little.

Toni walked into the kitchen, gave Eric a peck on the cheek, and then started talking to him in a soft voice. Ramona couldn't hear what she was saying. When she walked back by with the carryout containers for her last table, both of her parents were still talking to each other, but they were looking at her. Her mom had her eyebrows slightly raised and she wore a concerned look.

Great. Her mom must have heard that poor customer calling out to Ramona several times to get her attention.

"Let's go home and put our feet up,"

Toni said to Ramona as they headed back out to the dining area.

"It's okay, Mom. I can make it through the next forty-five minutes until my shift ends."

"Let's just go now," Toni said. "The rest of the staff can handle your tables until the evening shift shows up."

Ramona paused for a minute, trying to decide what would make her parents happier. Should she stay or go?

It seemed like her mom and dad were always making sacrifices for her and she wanted to repay them. Especially after she had to move back into their house with them after she caught pneumonia.

They were worried about her. She could see it on their faces. So, she swallowed the pride that made her want to prove she could stick it out and said, "Let me finish taking care of these customers and then we'll go."

Fifteen minutes later, the two of them

were walking out to Toni's sedan parked at the back of the diner's lot.

Ramona nervously scanned the parking lot and the nearby street. Things looked normal. Unless Darrin was perched atop one of the surrounding red brick buildings like some kind of sniper, she was probably safe. But despite the attempt to calm herself, she still felt exposed and vulnerable walking out in the open like this.

Toni started the engine and pulled the car out onto the street.

Exhausted, and really feeling it now that she was no longer working and pretending to be fine, Ramona tried to relax and sink back into the seat as her mom drove through town, but she couldn't. He body was tight with tension and she realized that some part of her was afraid to relax. In the back of her mind she felt like she had to stay on high alert and be ready to run for her life at any moment. Because the world was no longer the mostly sane, stable place that she'd believed it to be before last night's attack.

She rubbed her hands over her face and felt the small scratches on her cheeks and chin and forehead, etched there by the tree branches and pine needles as she'd fled through the forest. Her calf and thigh muscles were sore, too. She'd never been the kind of person who jogged for fun, so she was feeling the aftereffects this morning. At least her lungs weren't bothering her after all the running she'd done last night. That was a blessing.

She removed her hands from her face, gazing around at her familiar small town, grateful that the ride to her parents' house would be short.

Up ahead, the road dipped under a wide concrete railroad trestle. She and Jasmine used to ride their bikes down here when they were kids, enjoying the stomach-dropping thrill, even though their parents told them not to. Reaching this point meant that she was almost home. Maybe once she was inside the house, she'd be able to relax.

They were midway through the shadowy passage under the trestle when something hit their car from behind at high speed, striking with such force that the car jolted forward and started to spin out of their lane. When they emerged from the other side of the passage, they were facing the opposite direction and had moved into the opposing lane of traffic. Their car hit the grassy embankment and came to a sudden stop. The airbags deployed.

In the aftermath, Ramona sat there, stunned.

"Are you all right?" Toni asked as the airbags started to deflate.

Before Ramona could answer, a metal bar bashed through the window beside her repeatedly, breaking the glass and then clearing it away until a gloved hand reached through the void, unlocking the door and opening it.

Frantic, Ramona looked for her phone to call for help, but she couldn't find it before the gloved hand unfastened her seat belt, grabbed her arm and started pulling her out of the car.

Toni screamed and clutched Ramona's other arm, but the abductor was stronger—strong enough to pull Ramona out of her mother's grip.

A second assailant appeared, and like the first attacker, he wore a black ski mask that hid his face. He took hold of Ramona's free arm and together the men dragged her, kicking and screaming, toward a silver SUV that was parked at the top of the hill.

The car that had rear-ended them and caused the accident was still in the street, abandoned, with the driver's side door hanging open. One of the two men holding onto Ramona must have been driving it.

There wasn't usually much traffic in this part of town in the early afternoon and today was no exception. Nobody drove by who could help her. But even if there had been other people around, it probably wouldn't have mattered. Everything happened so quickly.

"Ramona!" She heard her mom yell her name, but she couldn't turn around to look at her. She fought with everything she had, but it didn't do any good. Even as her body heated up with the exertion of her struggles, her blood ran cold. Her abductors had to be Darrin Linder and one of his cronies.

Darrin was making good on his threat to silence her forever.

FOUR

Harry realized what was happening as soon as he spotted the car at an odd angle on the wrong side of the road. The sedan looked familiar. He'd seen it parked in the driveway of Ramona's house when he was there earlier that morning. It belonged to someone in her family.

And then his gaze fell on Ramona, twisting and thrashing as she was being dragged up the embankment beside the road, struggling to break free from the grip of a man with a knitted ski mask pulled down over his face. A second man, also masked, jumped into the driver's seat of an SUV at the top of the hill.

Oily anxiety swirled in the pit of Harry's stomach and his heart started pounding at a furious rate. Those men, one of whom had his hands on Ramona, were attempting to kidnap her. Harry could not let that happen.

Ramona's mom stood outside of the car, frantically waving at Harry with one hand while she held her phone up to her ear with the other. Police sirens wailed in the distance, but Harry knew they wouldn't arrive in time.

The jerk who was clutching Ramona moved fast, and he quickly wrestled her to the side of the SUV despite her struggles. He reached for the passenger side door handle as the SUV started rolling forward. Once he shoved Ramona inside, they would be gone. And Harry might not be able to catch up with them.

Determination and anger flared through his body as Harry floored the gas pedal in his truck, crossed the road and ploughed up the hill. His tires ripped up the grass and dirt as he headed straight for the SUV.

The trick would be to disable the SUV

without harming Ramona. And he only had a few seconds to figure it out.

His first thought was to aim for the front fender, driving into it with enough force to crumple the body of the vehicle and prevent it from moving any farther. But that would mean ramming the SUV close to the spot where Ramona was sitting. She could get hurt. So that was not a good option.

If he came to a stop in front of the SUV to block its escape, the driver could simply back up and drive around him. There was plenty of room.

Too soon, Harry was out of time. He had to commit to a plan *now*. Following his gut instincts, he eased off the accelerator and steered toward the back of the SUV.

As he drew closer, the creep clutching Ramona's arms turned to look in his direction and Ramona seized her opportunity. She jerked hard to her right, breaking free of the man's grip just before

Harry slammed into the SUV. Harry hit it harder than he intended and the impact caused the vehicle to spin clockwise, but that didn't matter. Ramona had gotten out of the way.

Harry could see Ramona running hard, skimming the top of the grassy hill and heading toward a nearby row of red brick town houses. The thug who'd had hold of her before was now hot on her heels—and gaining on her.

Harry threw his truck into Reverse and hit the gas, backing up a few feet and disentangling himself from the SUV. Then he shifted gears and spun the steering wheel, aiming for Ramona in the hope of getting to her before the bad guy did. But before he could hit the gas, the SUV revved up its engine and shot forward, hitting his truck's left front fender and blocking his pursuit before it even started.

Hot with frustration, Harry again reversed his truck to get away from the SUV. The wailing police sirens were getting louder so the cops must be closer. The driver of the SUV appeared to notice that, too. He gunned his engine, turned and sped off, driving across the grassy embankment until he hit blacktop. He shot down the road until he turned a corner, tires squealing, and disappeared into the surrounding neighborhood.

Harry turned his attention back to the direction where he'd last seen Ramona with the assailant chasing after her. He was too late. Both had already vanished from sight.

He steered across the grass toward the street, moving more cautiously as he tried to determine which path Ramona and her pursuer had taken.

Flashes of blue and red emergency lights reflected off his truck's mirrors and splashed through the cab's rear window. The wailing sirens suddenly stopped. The police must be on scene. A quick glance confirmed that two patrol cars had arrived and that officers were already talking to Ramona's mother.

Harry didn't have time to talk to the cops. Toni could do that. Instead, he said a quick prayer, asking for help and protection for Ramona as he turned down the street to the right of the town houses. The trees and shrubs along that road appeared thicker and there were more cars parked on the street. That meant more places to hide. If he were being pursued, that's the route he would choose.

He drove down the street, frantically looking for any sign of Ramona, until he got to the end. Nothing. And there was no one out on the street that he could question.

He must have made the wrong choice. A couple of quick turns took him to the other street he'd considered. Realistically she had to have run down one of them. Otherwise, he wouldn't have lost sight of her.

His windows were lowered and when

he was halfway down the road, he heard a commotion off to his right, where a narrow pedestrian passage cut between two houses and intersected with an alley. Several dogs were barking furiously in the surrounding yards and he heard a metallic crash that sounded like an industrial garbage container getting shoved against the side of a building.

Jumping on the possibility that was Ramona over there running for her life, Harry turned down the narrow passage, his truck barely fitting between the houses, and roared over to the intersecting alley.

He quickly realized that the so-called alley was less of a narrow service road and more of a parking lot when he barely avoided crashing into a faded orange-and-yellow motor home parked crosswise, leaving a gap too small for Harry's truck to fit through. He shoved the truck into Park, got out and took off on foot.

Harry spotted a man in faded jeans and

a green sweatshirt holding a broom and dustpan standing outside the open back door of an apartment building.

"Did somebody just run by here?" Harry demanded, grabbing the phone clipped to his belt and getting ready to call in the location to the police. "A woman with a man chasing after her?"

"Maybe." The guy shrugged. "I heard noises, but there's always something going on back here. I hardly pay attention it." He tightened his grip on the broom handle. "I didn't see anything."

Harry's jaw tensed in frustration. Maybe the guy hadn't seen anything. Or maybe he *had* but he didn't want to get involved. The second possibility was an aggravation Harry ran into on a fairly regular basis.

A sudden yelp, like the sound of someone in pain, snapped his attention away from the man. "Call the police!" he shouted as he started running down the alley.

The alley mirrored the turns of the curving roads in this part of town, so Harry couldn't see to the very end. There was a mixture of residences and businesses here. Shadowy pedestrian passages, like the one he'd driven through, branched off and led to streets on either side of him. Trash cans, wooden pallets and discarded cardboard boxes were stacked up behind some of the businesses. From the alley, it was impossible to see beyond them. For all Harry knew, Ramona could have run down one of those passages instead of staying to the main alleyway. She could be long gone.

Or she could be nearby, hiding, not realizing he was trying to save her.

Or—the most frightening possibility— the creep who'd been chasing her might have captured her. Made her hide with him behind some boxes or trash cans until the coast was clear. He could have a gun pressed to Ramona's head right now, forcing her to be silent until Harry passed them by.

The thought that she could be almost within reach, but he still might not be able to get to her to save her, unleashed a feeling of furious determination that Harry knew only too well.

His experience as a soldier had taught him to tamp down those emotions, to focus on the possibilities inherent to the situation at hand and quickly consider his actionable options. It was never easy, but it was the smart thing to do.

An image of Ramona's face, fearful yet determined as she'd sat in the Rock Solid Bail Bonds office, flashed through his mind. He thought of the bits of pine needle and twigs tangled in her dark hair, and the shadowed expression in her greenish-brown eyes. She'd been a combination of strength and fragility that made his heart ache. Made him want to protect her.

Stop.

She's not Willa.

If you ever truly loved your wife, how could you even consider replacing her with anyone else?

"Focus," Harry muttered, snapping his attention back to the alley.

So far, he hadn't called out Ramona's name because he was hoping to take advantage of the element of surprise. Best-case scenario—assuming the creep had Ramona—Harry would sneak up and capture him before the guy realized what was happening. But Harry felt like he had already wasted too much precious time in this search. The cops should arrive any minute. If the assailant was still in the vicinity, with Ramona as his hostage, the chance of sneaking up on him had come and gone.

Harry ran until he was past the final curve in the alley and stopped. He could see where the alley dead-ended at the back of the row of town houses. There was a red brick wall with a wrought-iron pedestrian gate left hanging open. On the other side of the gate was a small park. Could Ramona have gone through it?

In front of the brick wall were two more pedestrian passages, one on each side, leading out to the main streets on the left and right of the alley. At this point, it looked like Ramona and her pursuer could have gone anywhere.

Rather than give into despair, Harry spun around and decided to work from the assumption that she was still nearby.

"Ramona!" he yelled as loudly as he could while praying the police would hurry up and get there. With enough people, they could block all the exits off the alley and then search every inch of the area. If she wasn't there, they could send out media alerts and scour the entire town.

One thing was for certain, he would *not* give up on her.

He called out her name again and then listened carefully for a response. He didn't hear one.

As he grew increasingly worried, his heart thudded heavily in his chest. It was hard to believe she'd been in his life for less than twenty-four hours. He already felt a connection with her. Something beyond the straightforward fact that if he helped her and caught Linder, he would earn his fugitive recovery fee.

He continued walking quickly down the alley, looking around, fully aware that he was now making himself an easy target. Harry had a handgun, but he left it holstered. He would use it if he absolutely had to, but he'd rather not. There may not be people in the alley right now, but there were windows on the nearby stores and apartments and town houses, and he didn't want to risk hitting someone with a stray bullet.

He stopped and called out Ramona's name again. Almost immediately, a heavy truck rumbled down the adjacent road, drowning out every sound except for the deep, low growl of the engine. Just after that sound reached its loudest point and started to fade, Harry heard something.

It was up ahead, off the main alley. A metallic, rattling sound.

Harry started moving cautiously toward it, rounding the corner and stepping into a side passage. A neatly organized stack of pallets that he'd noticed as he passed earlier were now askew.

Sitting on the ground and squeezed between the pallets and a section of chain-link fence were Ramona and her captor. Ramona's foot was near the fence. She must have kicked it. That must have been the sound he heard.

Harry saw them before they realized he was there. Both of them were soaked in sweat, and the bad guy had pulled off his knit mask. Harry recognized him. He was the one Ramona called Skinny Guy when she'd described him to the police. He had Ramona pulled close to his right side, his arm wrapped around her shoulder and his hand clamped across her mouth. He held a gun in his other hand. And he kept glancing away from the direction of the alley, toward the street.

Harry heard approaching sirens. It felt like the police response had taken forever. But at least the guy outside the apartments had apparently called the police.

Harry pulled his weapon from his holster and quietly took a step back so he was hidden behind the corner of the building. The smartest thing would be to keep an eye on the two of them and wait for the cops to arrive. He could coordinate with the cops and make sure they caught the guy. Hopefully, they'd be able to get some information out of him that would take them closer to capturing Linder and ending the wave of violence he had started.

But it turned out Harry couldn't wait.

The silver SUV he'd battled with earlier suddenly appeared on the street at the end of the passage. It looked like the bald guy from the attack at the cabins last night was driving.

The criminal holding Ramona got to his feet and dragged her up with him. She moved slowly, obviously terrified and exhausted. But she still had enough fight left in her to not make things easy for Skinny Guy, twisting and turning and trying to wrench herself free from his grasp.

Harry had to admire the woman. She was no quitter.

Her efforts bought Harry enough time to move up quickly behind them. He was nearly close enough to jump on Skinny Guy and knock him to the ground when the thug must have heard his footsteps and spun around.

His eyes grew wide and he uttered a curse as he started to lift his pistol so that it was pointed directly at the side of Ramona's head.

"Stop!" Harry called out, aiming his gun at the man. "Don't move another inch or I *will* shoot you."

Ramona tried to scream, but the guy

still had his hand over her mouth. Her eyes grew wild with fear and her chest started heaving, like she was having trouble catching her breath.

Skinny Guy froze, a panicked expression on his face.

The police sirens were getting louder. The SUV driver impatiently gunned the engine.

Harry *really* wanted to catch these bad guys and lock them up. But more than that, he wanted Ramona to be safe. There was every reason to think this guy would shoot Ramona now if he thought he had to. Harry couldn't wait for the police. The situation was too volatile.

The SUV on the street started slowly moving forward. The driver obviously wasn't going to wait around until the cops arrived.

"Just let her go," Harry said.

And that's what Skinny Guy did, shoving Ramona at Harry while he turned and fled for the SUV.

Ramona stumbled and fell forward until Harry caught her just before she hit the pavement face first.

The SUV peeled out while Ramona started to sob uncontrollably.

Harry wrapped his arms around her. "You're okay," he said softly. "I've got you. You're safe."

Silently he prayed, *Thank You, Lord. Thank You.*

"If you think of anything else you want to tell me or if you remember any further detail from this attack, no matter how small, call me," Sergeant Bergman said.

He started to hand his business card to Ramona, but she wearily waved it away. "I still have your card from last night." Hard to believe it was just the previous night when this mess had started. When *she* had started it by going to Darrin's cabin at the Western Trails Resort. It already felt like a nightmare that had been going on for multiple days, or even weeks.

The sergeant was wrapping up his interview with her at her parents' house. The two of them had been sitting off in a corner where she'd just related the incidents of the attack for the fifth or sixth time as Bergman dug for any details she might have forgotten during the previous recitations. She'd also taken a look at some mug shots the sergeant had shown her on his tablet, hoping she could identify the two assailants working with Linder. Unfortunately, none of the men in the photographs looked familiar.

Ramona appreciated the cop's doggedness. The assailants had managed to get away and Bergman was trying to dig up every bit of information that might help them identify the two men.

She glanced over at her mom, who was calmly moving around the living room, making sure the visitors were comfortable. This, despite having been terrorized herself earlier when her car was bashed into and her daughter was kidnapped right in front of her.

The only sign of Toni's anxiety was when she would stop every now and then, take a deep breath, cross her arms over her chest and look around the room as if assessing the situation. Ramona often saw her do that at the diner when they were short-staffed and swamped with customers. It was how she calmed and centered herself.

Ramona's dad sat perched on the edge of a chair. He shifted his gaze back and forth between Ramona and Toni, looking like he was just waiting for the opportunity to jump up and do something for one of them.

A uniformed officer had accompanied Sergeant Bergman to the house. Cassie and Leon from the bail bonds office had arrived just a few minutes ago. And of course, Harry was there. He'd stayed within eyeshot even when they'd been separated for their police statements.

While it was comforting to know he was there, she was trying hard not to look at Harry. Whenever his gaze connected with hers, she found it nearly impossible to turn away.

He had saved her life. *Twice.* But what she felt toward him wasn't just gratitude. It was a tug of attraction. Allowing herself to be pulled in by that feeling was a very bad idea. The last thing Ramona needed right now was to be distracted by the bounty hunter helping her. She had problems she needed to focus on. *Serious* problems.

There were several moments today when she'd been certain her life was over. The masks worn by the thugs might have hidden their identity from any onlookers, but within a few seconds of being grabbed, Ramona had known exactly who they were—men who'd already tried to kill her once and wouldn't shy away from trying to again.

There'd been a few seconds in the alley

when she'd ducked behind an industrial trash can and thought she might have escaped, but Skinny Guy found her, dragging her out of sight and keeping the end of his pistol pressed to her temple while he called his partner to come get them.

The feeling of overwhelming fear from that moment came rushing back like a torrent even though she knew she was now safe at home. Her eyes began to burn and tears formed and rolled down her cheeks despite her efforts to blink them back. It horrified her to realize she'd been so overwhelmed while being held hostage in that dirty passageway she hadn't thought to pray.

But then Harry had showed up and everything was okay.

Not that she was complaining, but now that she thought about it, how was that possible?

"Why didn't one of those creeps just shoot me?" she wondered aloud.

Bergman looked at her for a moment,

the expression in his gray eyes hard to read. "Executing someone at point-blank range in broad daylight is very different from firing wildly at a vague figure in a dark forest," he said. "And it's risky. You never know when there's a witness around that you didn't see. Linder probably isn't paying them enough money to take that chance." He slipped his pen into his front pocket. "It's also possible that Linder's decided he wants you taken alive. Maybe use you as some kind of bargaining chip."

A few more tears rolled down Ramona's cheeks. She couldn't stop them.

The sergeant reached for a box of tissues on a nearby end table and handed it to her. "We're doing everything we can and using every available resource to find these thugs as quickly as possible." He stood and began to walk toward the door.

Ramona followed him. He stopped at the small entryway. "I probably don't have to say this, but don't go anywhere alone." He glanced toward her parents, who were now standing with their arms around one another. "It would be wise for her not to stay in the house alone, either."

Ramona cringed inwardly at the thought of her parents having to take more time away from the diner. Anytime one of them was away, it meant someone else had to be paid to take their place. And while the diner was successful, they still had to keep a close eye on costs.

"We'll be here to help protect Ramona," Cassie spoke up. So far, she and Leon had mostly sat quietly, sipping the coffee that Eric had given them.

Ramona was surprised by the bondswoman's comment. She thought Cassie had come to listen to details about the case that could help in her pursuit of Darrin Linder. Which was perfectly reasonable. She hadn't expected Cassie to offer her protection.

Bergman glanced at Cassie and nodded. "I'm glad to know you'll be helping her.

And I'm not surprised." He said his good-byes and left with the uniformed officer.

"I live on a horse ranch with husband-and-wife caretakers, Jay and Sherry Laughlin," Cassie said after Bergman was gone. She shifted her gaze to include Ramona and her parents. "Jay used to be a cop until he got injured on the job. Sherry is a veterinary technician, which is helpful since the main focus of the ranch these days is boarding horses. My dad, Adam, also lives at the ranch. He founded Rock Solid Bail Bonds and worked there until a couple years ago when he retired—kind of. The truth is he can't keep his hands out of the business. Somebody's always around, so you wouldn't have to worry about being alone, and all of us are armed and capable of providing some protection. Plus, the place has pretty good security due to the business I'm in. Please, come and stay with us."

"I'll be there, too," Harry said quietly,

moving so that he was standing beside Ramona.

Ramona looked at him and felt a familiar fluttering her in stomach when their gazes met. Later, when she was stronger, she would find a way to make that feeling stop.

"Maybe you should stay home," Toni said. "In case you get sick again and need me to take care of you."

"Sick?" Harry asked, looking ashen.

Ramona sighed. "I had pneumonia recently. A bad bout that took a few months to clear up. I have asthma, too, which might be why things got so bad so quickly. That's the reason I had to move out of Jasmine's condo and come back home. I couldn't keep working to chip in money to help Jasmine with her mortgage payments. I figured that if I moved out, she'd find someone else to move in and help out. Plus, there was a stretch of time when I could barely get out of bed and I did need a lot of help. Sometimes exertion, like running, makes my lungs ache. But otherwise I'm healed up and fine, now."

"*Mostly* healed up," her mom said quietly.

Ramona glanced at Harry, but he was no longer looking in her direction. She walked over to her parents. "I think spending a few days at Cassie's ranch until Darrin and those other two jerks are captured and all of this is over is a good idea. It sounds very secure."

Her mom sighed but finally, reluctantly, nodded. Her dad cleared his throat and also gave an affirming nod.

Ramona blew out a sigh of relief. Staying here at the house would only continue to put her parents in harm's way and she wasn't going to do that anymore. The people at Cassie's ranch sounded like they were ready for anything. And she knew she could count on Harry.

Maybe if she stayed there with the bounty hunters, she'd have more opportunities to answer questions and help them with their pursuit. She had to do everything she could. The situation was already frighteningly out of hand. And Darrin Linder had shown he was capable of anything.

FIVE

If she weren't in fear for her life, Ramona might have been able to enjoy the sunrise the following morning at North Star Ranch.

Not that her life appeared to be in danger right this very moment. It was just that after everything that happened the previous afternoon, plus all that happened the night before at the cabins, she was starting to wonder about how much of a future she truly had. And that fear ran the risk of distracting her from the natural beauty of the mountains and forest in front of her.

If Darrin managed to find her, if her life ended right this moment, would the

Lord be disappointed in her and the life choices she'd made?

Her parents had encouraged her to pursue a career in accounting like her Aunt Valerie. To have a stable income and do something significant with her life. Wanting to make them happy, she started down that path a year ago, taking classes part time while working for a financial firm in town. She'd dressed for success in suits and heels and started making the personal connections that could help her future career.

But during that time, she'd missed working at the diner. She missed chatting with the retired customers who were there every morning like clockwork. And she missed the clusters of awkward high school kids who showed up in the afternoon, trying to behave like adults as they studied the menu and then later spent an inordinate amount of time with their heads together trying to figure out how much to leave for a tip.

She'd lost her job at the financial firm when she came down with pneumonia and had to miss so much work. After she healed, she'd gone back to working at the diner. It had felt like home.

She'd been so happy to be back, even if she felt guilty, knowing it wasn't where her parents wanted her to be. They loved their diner, but it was hard work, the hours were long, and they were on their feet constantly. It didn't generate a huge profit, and the money that did come in was unevenly distributed throughout the year. They did pretty well around holidays and throughout the summer; the rest of the year, their income was hit or miss.

Eric and Toni told Ramona they wanted more for her. More money. More prestige. More free time to enjoy herself. They wanted her to have a life like Aunt Valerie, Jasmine's mom, who had done well for herself and had convinced Jasmine to follow in her footsteps. Yes, there were times when Valerie was very busy at work, but it wasn't *all* the time. And she was well paid.

Ramona wondered if she had the right to choose working at the diner, and perhaps buying it from her parents one day, over the business career they hoped she'd have. Would any sane person opt for working on her feet all day for an uncertain income over working in an office cubicle for a steady paycheck? Would she be burying whatever humble talents she'd been blessed with if she didn't choose the path that appeared more stable and financially rewarding?

But then again, did any of this matter if she might lose her life at any moment?

She closed her eyes, feeling the burden of the last two days weighing especially heavy on her shoulders. *Dear Lord, please protect all of us. Please help us find Darrin Linder and his criminal companions and bring them to justice. And please help me to know Your will for my life.*

She opened her eyes and shivered

slightly as she crossed her arms and wrapped her heavy, cable-knit sweater tighter across her body. The sun had risen a little higher and golden light spilled across the small valley. Several of the horses being boarded at the ranch were already turned out into the corral. They trotted around calmly, stopping to sniff the light breeze every now and then, their steps sure and firm as they kicked up a little of the raked dirt in the enclosure.

A dappled gray Appaloosa caught Ramona's eye as it stopped and chuffed deeply a couple of times, its exhalations leaving wispy clouds in the cool air.

Ramona heard the door to the ranch house open and shut behind her. She turned around to see Cassie walking the gravel path in her direction, a coffee mug in each hand. Eventually Cassie made it to the stretch of split rail fencing where Ramona had been standing, gazing at the surrounding mountaintops and thick pines.

It had been pitch-black when Ramona arrived at the ranch last night in Harry's truck. After an anxious night spent tossing and turning, she'd finally decided to get outside for some fresh air, hoping it might help calm her down. So far, it hadn't really helped.

One of the horses in the corral whinnied loudly, tossing its head back a couple of times, just as Cassie stepped alongside Ramona and offered her a mug. "I put in a little cream and sugar."

"That's perfect, thank you." The rich aroma of coffee offered comfort and the possibility of calming Ramona's nerves. It took a measure of self-control to keep from snatching it out of Cassie's hand. The first sip was delicious and seemed to straighten her spine a little. The second sip was even better.

"Taffy isn't a boarder, she lives here." Cassie gestured with her mug toward the chestnut mare that had started whinnying and now moved toward the edge of the corral closest to Cassie. "Dad bought her for me as a birthday present years ago. She's probably worried to see me up so early," she joked.

The animal hung her head over the railing and gave Cassie an adoring look with her chocolate-brown eyes. Cassie ambled over to talk to her and give her a few pats and vigorous scratches on her neck and cheek and forehead.

"How'd you sleep last night?" Cassie asked, walking back to Ramona.

Ramona hesitated. Admitting that she'd tossed and turned all night might make her sound ungrateful. "The room is very comfortable," she finally said. "And you've got a beautiful ranch. Thank you again for inviting me here."

Cassie took a sip of coffee and nodded. "You didn't sleep a wink, did you?"

Ramona sighed and shook her head. "Everything that happened yesterday kept playing through my mind." And she couldn't stop herself from imagining the terrible things that might have happened if Harry hadn't found her in time.

"I understand how that goes," Cassie said. "Trauma isn't something you can just work through in a day. But over time, things often do get better."

"You said your horse was surprised to see you," Ramona said after a sip of coffee, eager to change the subject. "Does that mean you're not a morning person?"

Cassie laughed and shook her head. "No. I'm definitely not a morning person."

In jeans and a flannel shirt, with no makeup, she looked very young. But there was a weary expression in her eyes, evidence that she'd lived through a lot. On the ride to the ranch last night with Harry, Ramona had learned that while Cassie had chosen to continue to use the surname of Wheeler in her professional life, she was a widow and her husband had been murdered. The crime was still unsolved.

"It's the nature of the bail bonds business that if you go looking for bail jumpers and informants," Cassie went on, "you're probably going to find them visiting their favorite haunts around midnight."

"If they're out late, why don't you just go to their home around midday when they're probably still asleep and arrest them then? Wouldn't that be easier?"

Cassie arched a slender strawberry-blond eyebrow. "If they actually reside at the location they give us as their home address, recovering them is typically not a big deal. Those are the people who intended to do right but slipped up. Maybe they lost track of when they were supposed to appear in court. Or they intended to get sober and didn't. They made a bad decision. There are a lot of reasons for that happening.

"Then there are the people who are deliberately trying to hide. People who knew from the beginning that they were going to jump bail. That type will give us bad information on their bond application. We do what we can to corroborate it all, but the nature of the business is that you aren't always dealing with people who have a stable address. Typically, we track them down by going to places where they like to hang out and socialize. And most of those places don't start to come alive until well into the evening."

Ramona gave her a half smile. "So, you're here right now because you actually got to bed at a decent hour last night and figured you'd take advantage of a rare day when you could roll out of bed early and greet the morning?"

Cassie chuckled. "Hardly." She hooked her thumb toward the stables where someone had obviously been working since before Ramona first stepped outside. "My dad called me and woke me up. He and Jay are in there working. I'm pretty sure Harry's with them. Dad saw you out here and wanted me to make sure you were

okay. Plus, Sherry's cooking a big breakfast this morning. Belgian waffles with
huckleberries and whipped cream. Dad
knew I wouldn't want to miss that."

Cassie's father, a long-time widower,
had greeted Ramona when she'd arrived
at the ranch last night. Ramona had also
met Jay and Sherry Laughlin, the married couple who took care of the ranch.
From them, she learned that along with
being a boarding and training facility for
the general public, North Star also main-
tained close ties to equestrian search-and-
rescue associations.

"Belgian waffles sound great," Ramona
said. "And I appreciate everyone looking
out for me."

Cassie scuffed the toe of a boot in the
dirt. "Yeah, well, just know it's not a
vacation and we're going to put you to
work."

Ramona smiled and realized her mood
had started to lighten a little. "Of course.
I'll muck out stables or gather eggs out

of the chicken coop. Whatever you need. I'm happy to earn my keep."

"If you want to do any of that, go for it. But what I had in mind is getting your help to track Linder and his cronies. I'm hoping the cops will capture them quickly and get them off the streets, but in the meantime, we're going to do what we can to help. We might not have the technology available to the police, but professional bounty hunters like Harry, Leon, Martin and me, people who focus full time on tracking people for a living, develop a strong sense for what we're doing."

"Martin?" Ramona said. She'd heard his name mentioned before, at the bail bonds office, but she hadn't met him—at least, she didn't think she had. The first hour or so after Harry had rescued her yesterday was a blur. "Have I met Martin?"

"Not yet, but you will."

Ramona heard a chime. Cassie pulled

a phone out of her jeans pocket, glanced at it, then tucked the phone away.

"I can't tell you much about Darrin," Ramona said. "I only knew him because he was Jasmine's boyfriend."

"His bond application gives an Olympia, Washington, address for his parents. Do you know if that's where he's from?"

"He said his company transferred him over here from Olympia. And I've heard him mention that his parents still live over on the Washington coast."

Cassie nodded. "I think I'll send Leon and Martin over there to talk to them."

"Jasmine might have their phone number so you can just call," Ramona offered.

Cassie shook her head. "I'll take the number to see if it matches what we have on file. But I'm still going to send the guys over there. Most people find it harder to lie to your face than over the phone. And no matter what they say, it's more informative if you can see them for yourself and read their body language."

Her phone chimed again. She looked at the screen and sighed. "I'm getting texts from an impatient bail bondsman out of Miami who needs some help. He's got a couple of jumpers he's looking for and his informants tell him they lit out for Idaho or Montana." A half smile settled on her face. "It's always fun to capture the big-city criminals who think they're going to come out here to hide."

"Go ahead and take care of business," Ramona said. "Maybe I'll go talk to the horses."

Cassie tapped the screen on her phone and then held it up to her ear. "Yeah, Harry, I'm out here in front of the house with Ramona. I've got to go back inside and get some work done. Why don't you come out here and keep her company until Sherry says breakfast is ready? Good." She disconnected.

A minute or so later Harry walked out of a stable door and when Ramona saw him her heart did a slow somersault in her chest. She *had* to find a way to make that stop. By the time he reached her, Cassie was already talking on her phone to the bondsman in Miami and heading into the house.

"You look like you're used to ranch work," Ramona said to Harry. Her heart was racing and her words came out sounding breathy, which was embarrassing. Standing in a beam of early-morning sunlight, with a little bit of straw in his hair, he looked ridiculously handsome. Having his shirtsleeves rolled up, exposing his muscular arms, made it even worse.

"I *am* used to it," he said. "I grew up on the family cattle ranch. I still help out when they need me to."

He moved a little closer and his glittering blue eyes held her like a tractor beam. She willed herself to look away, but she just couldn't. A smile formed on his lips and she realized he was aware of the effect he was having on her.

Well, that was just annoying.

And it turned out that being annoyed gave her just enough gumption to finally look away. She focused her gaze on the corral and on Cassie's horse-friend, Taffy. "Yesterday before the attack, the text you sent said you had some questions for me and Jasmine," she said to Harry without looking at him.

"Mainly, I had a question *for* you *about* Jasmine."

That got her attention and she turned to look at him, determined to maintain her emotional distance this time. "Okay. What's the question?"

"Yesterday morning, I went to Darrin's former workplace, Earth Movers Equipment. Their vice president came down to the lobby to speak with me. He told me that they would only provide personal information about Darrin to law enforcement. And that the Stone River PD had already been in contact with them."

"What does that have to do with Jasmine?"

"After I left the building, a man came out a minute or two later and caught up with me. His name was Karl Bock and he said he was a salesman there, like Darrin. He overheard my conversation in the lobby with the vice president. He gave me the names of some places Darrin liked to hang out when they worked together. Some restaurants, bars, that sort of thing. Places where he thought Darrin might go if he's still in town. Which is helpful. Even if Darrin doesn't show up at any of those places, we might get some useful information from one of the regulars."

"That's good," Ramona said, still wondering how this was going to relate to Jasmine.

"Karl told me about seeing Darrin and Jasmine having dinner together just four or five days ago." Harry watched Ramona closely. "That would have her still dating Darrin much more recently than she's claimed. So, I have to ask you, how certain are you that Jasmine and Darrin are really broken up?"

Ramona's stomach dropped. And then her face got hot.

Harry held up his hands in a placating gesture. "I'm not accusing. And I'm not judging. I won't even pretend to understand the dynamics of an abusive relationship. But is it possible that she's still in the on-again, off-again stage? That she hasn't completely broken things off with him yet?"

"You think Jasmine would stay involved with a man who tried to kill me?" Ramona snapped.

"This dinner would have been before the first attack on you, but after Darrin had threatened your family. I am asking you what you think."

"I think Karl was lying or misremembering," Ramona said defensively, even if a small part of her wondered if that were true. Jasmine was not a cruel or uncaring person. Far from it. And Ramona knew Jasmine truly cared about her. But she had issues that sometimes got in the way of making good decisions. She'd made promises to Ramona and then broken them before. Maybe she'd broken her promise to stop seeing Darrin. Maybe she hadn't really been able to stop using drugs.

"I want to go back and talk to her again this evening after she gets home from work," Harry said.

Ramona crossed her arms. "I'm going with you."

"I counted on that."

The sound of dogs barking caught Ramona's attention. Cassie's dad, a sinewy man with a shock of thick silver hair, was walking over from the stables with a couple of excited mutts bounding around at his feet. The dogs were a ridiculous sight, with one nearly the size of a Great Dane and the other not much bigger than a Yorkie.

"I got a text from Sherry. Breakfast is

ready," he called out when he got close to them. "We need to get to the kitchen before all the waffles are gone."

Ramona didn't have much of an appetite with all of the worries on her mind and knots in her stomach, but she knew she needed to keep up her strength. If this day was anything like the two that had come before it, she'd need to fuel up to be ready.

But what could she eat or drink to strengthen her for confronting her cousin? Maybe she'd expected too much from Jasmine too quickly. Maybe the truth was she and her cousin were both in serious danger.

"What was the man's name?" Jasmine asked Harry. "The man who said he saw me having dinner with Darrin just a few days ago. Because that's not true." She shoved her fisted hands onto her hips.

They had only been in Jasmine's condo for a minute or two, not even long enough for them to sit down, when Ramona confronted Jasmine about the man's comment.

Harry reached for his phone. "His name is Karl. I've forgotten his last name. Let me look at my notes."

Jasmine rolled her eyes. "You don't need to. Tall guy with dark hair, right? Looks like he stepped out of a men's cologne ad?"

The man had in fact been stylishly dressed in an expensive-looking suit. "Yes," Harry said.

"Karl Bock." Jasmine let out a scoff of irritation. "Figures. He was Darrin's main rival. They run contests there and pay substantial bonuses based on hitting certain sales targets. Karl won nearly every contest until Darrin showed up and gave him some competition. Stole the limelight from old golden boy Karl."

"I understand there being bad blood between them, but why would this guy lie about *you*?" Ramona interjected.

Jasmine shook her head and dropped onto the sofa in her living room, arms crossed tightly over her chest and her cheeks turning red. "I saw Karl a few times at the Earth Movers office and at work-related social events when I was still with Darrin. When Darrin wasn't looking, Karl flirted with me. I could tell it wasn't anything personal, it was just part of his attempt to compete with Darrin. He was trying to steal me away. He asked me out, more than once, and I turned him down each time. I could tell it bruised his ego."

"Maybe Karl just misjudged the timing of how recently he'd seen you and Darrin together," Harry said, trying to tone down the tension in the room. Ramona was stressed and frustrated with her cousin, and Jasmine was defensive. Letting things become confrontational was not going to get Harry the information he needed.

"I'm *not* lying," Jasmine said defiantly

to Ramona. Then she sniffed loudly and her eyes started to tear up. "This is all my fault." She swiped her eyes. "Mom and I were so upset when we heard what happened to you yesterday. Did your parents tell you we wanted to come over to their house and see you? But they thought it was a bad idea."

"Yes, they did tell me." Ramona sat down on the sofa next to her cousin and took her hand.

Jasmine started crying all the harder. "I have something to tell you but I'm afraid you won't believe me," she said. "Especially now."

Harry sat down in a chair across from her and watched her closely.

"What is it?" Ramona asked.

Jasmine gulped in a deep breath. Then she dug her phone out of her purse and showed them a text: No one will ever come between us.

"Did this come from Darrin's number?" Harry asked.

"I've never seen this number before."

"When did you get it?"

"Late last night."

"Why didn't you tell me when I called you this morning to tell you we were coming over?" Ramona asked, her tone indignant.

"Because I know what my track record is and I didn't think you'd believe me if I told you I'm not doing anything at all to encourage him. I don't want him back. *Especially* after what he's done to you." Jasmine's head dropped down and she looked at the floor as she continued talking. "And I want you to know I've got meetings set up with a counselor. I haven't been using any drugs at all for a while, now." She lifted her head and looked Ramona in the eyes. "That's the truth. But I'm scared. I've failed before. So, this time I'm doing things right. I'm checking in with the counselor every single day."

"I'm glad to hear that," Ramona said,

wrapping her arm around her cousin's shoulder for a side hug. "And I believe that you broke up with Darrin for good a couple of weeks ago like you said you did."

"You should let the cops know about that text," Harry said. "They might be able to trace it. Or get a billing address attached to the account and find Darrin that way."

"Okay."

Ramona dug Sergeant Bergman's card out of her wallet and handed it to her cousin. Jasmine punched in the number. Within a few seconds, she was nervously pacing back and forth between the living room and the kitchen while talking to Bergman.

After a few moments, Harry turned to Ramona. Seeing her this morning at the ranch, he'd thought about how vibrant and strong she looked, especially considering all she'd been through. Looking at her in that golden sunlight, he never would have thought she'd had health issues. Battling pneumonia, that was serious business.

But then Willa had looked vibrant and strong the last morning he'd seen her. An hour later, he'd received the call that she'd collapsed. And just before midnight, his wife was declared dead. The brain aneurysm and resultant complications had snatched away her life.

Harry forced his thoughts back to the situation at hand. He glanced at Jasmine, who was still on the phone. "Do you honestly believe what she just told us?" he asked Ramona. He wasn't entirely convinced. Maybe Jasmine had seen Darrin more recently but she was embarrassed to admit it.

"I do," Ramona answered. "And I believe Darrin knows she's taking steps to heal. That's why he's pursuing me and tormenting her—because he knows that his chance to get her back is slipping away. She's going back to church. Her faith is growing stronger. He can't manip-ulate her or control her with drugs any-more. And he's panicking."

Faith. It had pulled Harry back from the edge of an emotional abyss more than once. First in the military, when he'd seen so many horrible things in combat. And then after Willa's sudden death.

He hadn't faced the exact same chal-lenges that Jasmine was going through, but he'd dealt with his own version. And who was he to judge her? Recovery and healing were not straight-line kinds of things. They were typically zigzags. That was true whether you were talking about recovery from addiction, recovery from a bad relationship or recovery from a dev-astating loss.

Life could be harrowing. And Harry was grateful for the faith his parents had raised him with. What would he have done without it?

Jasmine came back from the kitchen. "The police are going to do what research they can with the phone number," she said, setting her phone down onto a table.

"Do you think you're in danger?" Ramona asked and then glanced over at Harry. "Do you think you need to move somewhere else until all this is over?"

Harry met the questioning look in Ramona's eyes and gave a single nod. If Jasmine wanted to come out to the ranch, he would work that out with Cassie.

Jasmine shook her head. "I'm being careful. I have friends going with me to and from work. And Alex is coming by tomorrow with his work crew to finally put in a security system. He said he's decided to put one in all of the condos he's built. Just to be safe."

Ramona nodded. "I'm glad to hear that."

Jasmine sat back down on the couch beside Ramona. "You're the one who's in danger." She patted Ramona's hand. "I'm sorry to say it, but it's true."

Harry had come to the same, glaringly

obvious conclusion. Based on the text message, it seemed Darrin thought Ramona was trying to come between him and Jasmine. And he would do whatever was necessary to keep that from happening.

Harry glanced over at Ramona. She gave him a brave, encouraging smile that made his heart ache just a little. And he realized he'd try just about anything anyone suggested to keep her safe.

Jasmine cleared her throat and turned to Harry. "So, I heard a few people at the office today talking about going over to the lounge at the Water Grill after work for a couple of drinks. That reminded me of when Darrin used to go there to hang out with some of his friends. Maybe you could find someone there who knows something about him that can help you."

Harry glanced at Ramona. "I'll get you back to the ranch and then I'll go check it out."

"I don't think you have time for that,"

Jasmine said, shaking her head. "They have a free appetizer buffet and drink specials from five to seven. After that, most of the happy hour crowd clears out. I don't know exactly where the ranch is, but it's obviously out of town. It's already after six, right now. By the time you drop her off and get to the lounge, the people you want to talk to would be gone."

"I'll go with you," Ramona said to Harry. "It'll be okay. I don't imagine Darrin will actually be there. Whatever friends he used to have there must know he's a wanted man. It's a nice, upscale place. If any of the employees see him, they'll call the police. He's got to know that."

Ramona's reasoning was solid. The problem was, Harry wasn't sure Darrin would behave in a reasonable way. Heading to the lounge with her was a risk. But letting things continue any longer was a risk, too.

Sometimes in order to make a capture,

Harry had to take a chance. He just hated doing it when it was someone else's safety he was putting on the line. But what other choice did he have?

SIX

"I came here to the Water Grill for dinner with colleagues a couple of times back when I was working my office job downtown," Ramona said. "I've heard about their Thursday night happy hour, but I never checked it out for myself. It's not exactly my scene."

Harry pulled his truck into a slot in the restaurant's parking lot. "So, what is your scene?" His tone had a slight edge of teasing to it.

Good question, Ramona thought. What was her *scene*? Did she even have one?

No, not really.

But admitting that would probably make her sound pitiful to him. He was a bounty hunter who was also a combat veteran. No doubt his scene involved doing something impressive, like wrestling steers or rescuing hostages. She decided to ignore his question and reach for the door handle.

He immediately threw his arm in front of her. Momentum had her pressing into it before she realized what was happening and once again there was no missing Harry Orlansky's muscles. Wherever his scene was, the women who inhabited it probably flocked to him like flies on honey. There was no denying that he was a handsome man. And he could be charming when he wanted to be.

"Let's just sit here for a minute," he said after he dropped his arm back down, the earlier hint of playfulness in his voice replaced by a more serious tone. He glanced around at the other vehicles and people in the parking lot, and then checked the truck's side and rearview mirrors.

"Do you really think we were followed?" Ramona asked, twisting in her seat and looking out the windows beside and behind her.

"I wouldn't say it's likely, but it is possible," Harry answered. "I'd rather be cautious than take a chance when I don't have to. So, let's just sit here and watch the people and vehicles around us for a few minutes."

"All right." Ramona settled back into her seat.

"So, we were talking about *your* scene," Harry said. "Tell me about it. What do you like to do for fun?"

Great, they were back to that. "What do you do?" she countered.

"When I'm not chasing bail jumpers, I'm usually working on my parents' ranch. And I volunteer with an equine search-and-rescue group. That's how I met Cassie and her dad. After my wife passed away, I was pretty lost and aimless." His voice became husky with emotion. "After about six months of that, Adam offered to train me to work as a bounty hunter. He told me it would give me a sense of purpose and help take my mind off my sorrows. He was right. It might not be therapeutic for most people, but it was the perfect thing for me."

Harry was a widower. Ramona felt a pang of heartache in sympathy for him. She couldn't imagine the grief he had gone through.

"I'm not interested in bars or social scenes or anything like that," he added. "Well-intentioned friends have tried to drag me to places where I could meet new people. I know they were trying to give me a push back into dating, but that's not for me." He shook his head. "I'm not looking to get married again."

It was ridiculous that Ramona was stung with disappointment at his words. Hadn't she already told herself that he wasn't the stable, low-drama kind of guy she was looking for?

"Your turn," Harry said, as he watched a trio of men get out of an SUV and walk toward the restaurant's entrance. "Tell me about yourself."

Why? was her initial thought.

It was possible he was open to being friends. Or maybe he was just bored. In any event, he'd been willing to open up a little bit so it seemed only fair that she should, too.

"When I was a teenager, I used to help my parents at the diner," Ramona said. Just a few minutes ago, she'd been worried about her life seeming boring and pitiful to him considering the exciting life he must live. But now that she knew how deeply he was mourning, that concern just seemed childish and petty.

They weren't on a date. It didn't matter what he thought. Admittedly, she found him attractive, but he'd just told her he wasn't looking for another special woman in his life. And rather than try to *help* him or fix his problems for him, she was going to believe him and move on. While she was battling pneumonia, she'd made a promise to herself that she was going to stop repeating the same unhealthy decisions she'd made in the past when it came her relationships. And she was going to keep that promise. No more trying to win over men with relationship issues. Of any sort. That was a dead end.

And since she was already way too drawn to Harry, it would probably be best for her peace of mind to keep her distance from him altogether, once it was safe for them to part ways. Even worse than a relationship that was going nowhere would be a relationship that was one-sided, with her pining over an unavailable man.

When the hunt for Darrin and his accomplices was over, that would have to be the end of any budding friendship between Ramona and Harry. So, that being the case, why shouldn't she be honest with Harry right now? Why not tell him about her embarrassingly uneventful life?

"I put in a lot of hours working at Kitchen Table and I liked it," she continued. "I enjoyed chatting with the regulars. I liked moving all the time instead of sitting at a desk even if it made me tired by the end of the day. My parents wanted me to pursue a professional career working in an office like my Aunt Valerie so I'd have a larger, more stable income than they did and maybe have an easier life. I tried that for a year and a half. I worked at a finance company and took business classes at night, until I came down with pneumonia and couldn't work or attend school at all for three months. In some ways, it was actually a relief. I didn't like the office job. I don't want to sit at a desk and stare at a computer screen all day." There, she'd finally said that out loud to someone. Maybe eventually she'd be able to say it to her parents.

"Our church has a ministry where we bring meals to people who are homebound and I spend time with them when I can. It's not a big deal," she continued, feeling a little self-conscious for mentioning it. But she wanted him to know that she did have a life. It just wasn't one that would impress very many people. "I drop off some food from the diner and hang out for a half hour or so, chatting with people or sometimes just listening to someone who's been home alone all day."

"That's a pretty cool scene," Harry said.

"Yeah, right," Ramona shot back. Obviously, the big bad bounty hunter was making fun of her.

"Sounds like you've found something you enjoy doing for a living. Not everybody can say that. And it sounds like you know how to talk to people, even strangers, and give them an encouraging word. Maybe the only kind word they hear all day. Not everybody can do that. I know *I* can't do that." He shook his head. "Half the time what I say makes people feel worse instead of better. I'm the king of sticking my foot in my mouth. Just ask my family."

Ramona couldn't help laughing a little.

At the same time, she felt a little sting of heartache. Because Harry got it. Without her explaining, he understood what it was about the things she liked to do that made them important to her and made her happy.

But her *scene* was so simple. Was it too simple? Was she doing enough with her life? Or by not being more ambitious, was she not fully using the talents she'd been given? *Lord, I need Your guidance about so many things right now,* she prayed silently.

"All right, let's go," Harry said.

They climbed out of his truck and headed into the main entrance. The Water Grill was built on the edge of Lake Bell, and as soon as they stepped inside, they were greeted with a view of the water through the floor-to-ceiling window on the far side of the building. There was still enough daylight to see slightly rippling water and the dusky shadows beneath the tall pines on the shoreline as dark clouds started rolling in. To the right of the foyer was the bar and lounge with its cozy furniture groupings and oversize fireplace. To the left was the entrance to the restaurant.

Harry held Ramona's arm with a light touch and steered her toward the bar. "First stop is the bartender," he said softly into her ear. "The good ones know all the regulars, all the gossip and everything that happens in their establishment."

"Have you talked to this guy before?" Ramona asked, glancing toward the man with short red hair and sideburns behind the bar.

"Nope."

As they approached the bar, the bartender smoothly moved toward them. "What'll you have?"

"Just some information." Harry held up his phone to show him a photo of Darrin Linder. "Have you seen this man?"

The bartender made a scoffing sound. "I keep up with the news. If Darrin Linder showed up in here, I'd call the cops." His gaze lingered on Ramona for a few seconds and she swallowed thickly. Was it possible the man was lying? Maybe he was part of Darrin's drug distribution business. As soon as she turned away, would he take out his phone and call Darrin to tell him that Ramona was here?

Finally, the bartender shook his head slightly. "You look like the woman who used to come in with him once in a while, but now I can see that you aren't her."

That would be my cousin, Ramona thought. But she didn't say anything.

"What can you tell me about Darrin?" Harry asked. "Did he ever talk about other places he liked to go or what he liked to do? Was there someone he usually met when he came in?"

"Look, he didn't come in and sit at the bar and talk to me. Or even talk in front of me." The bartender gestured with his chin toward the people settled in the plush chairs near the fireplace. "He was here to talk with the other suits. Network with them and make business contacts. That's what Thursday night happy hour is designed for. You might want to talk to one of the cocktail servers. They'd be more likely to have overheard something."

Harry questioned each of the two cocktail servers as they walked up to the bar to place their orders. Neither one could provide any helpful information about Darrin other than to confirm that he wasn't in the lounge right now and that neither one had seen him since he quit his job at Earth Movers shortly before he was arrested for selling drugs.

"Let's head over to the fireplace," Harry said to Ramona after he thanked the servers. "And when we get there...normally, I'm an 'honesty is the best policy' kind of guy, but sometimes bounty hunters, like cops, need to lie in order to do their job."

"So, you're saying we're not telling them that you're a bounty hunter and we're looking for Darrin?"

"Not at first. We'll see how things go."

She nodded. "All right, I understand." Like Harry, she valued honesty. But tracking down Darrin was an extraordinary situation. Not only was her life in danger, but her family's was, too. Beyond that, there was the potential damage he could do to the community as a result of his drug distribution and his recent expansion into illegal gun sales.

They walked up to a small table and sat down. Immediately a voice called out, "Hey, it's the bounty hunter."

A dark-haired man walked toward them and Harry blew out a quick puff of air in frustration before whispering, "It's Karl. The man who followed me out of Earth Movers to talk to me."

Ramona kept her eye on the man. This was the guy who'd claimed he'd seen Jasmine with Darrin within the last five days. It was tempting to give him a piece of her mind for lying about her cousin. But now was not the time or place for that. They were here to get information from the people in the lounge, not set them on edge.

And if she were completely honest with herself, Ramona couldn't say that she one hundred percent believed Jasmine. Yes, her cousin was working very hard right now to get her life back on track. But Jasmine didn't have a history of being a completely stable person. And Ramona knew any significant life change usually involved some backsliding before a person could get solidly settled on their new path.

Maybe Jasmine had backslid with Darrin and gone back to him for a short time. At this point it felt like anything was possible.

"You two are bounty hunters?" a woman at a nearby table asked with a smile on her face. Her glance took in both Ramona and Harry. Her companions looked intrigued, as did the people at two other nearby tables who'd apparently overheard.

Before Ramona could explain that she wasn't actually a bounty hunter, Harry was already taking advantage of the situation. He started asking questions and the happy hour patrons seemed eager to help. A couple of them had actually worked with Darrin, while the rest knew him as a Thursday night regular. And while three or four vocalized their disbelief that Darrin's life had taken such a dramatic and violent turn, Ramona couldn't help noticing the others who kept quiet and exchanged subtle glances with one another.

Maybe they, like Ramona, had sensed something off about Darrin before he got arrested. Maybe they, too, sensed that growing undercurrent of violence in his behavior.

Jasmine had taken forever to admit to seeing it. By the time she finally got around to telling Ramona that he'd knocked her to the ground—more than

once—Ramona hadn't been at all surprised to hear it. Horrified but not surprised. Thankfully, once Jasmine had
taken that first step of admitting the problem out loud, Ramona had been able to
convince her to report it to the police.
That was the beginning of getting Jasmine out of that horrible relationship and
to a safer environment.

In the weeks since then, Darrin had
gone completely off the rails and proven
Ramona's intuition was correct.

To Ramona's disappointment, she didn't
hear anyone in the lounge offer a tip for
finding Darrin. No one claimed friendship with him or admitted to spending
time with him anywhere other than at
the bar or at his workplace. So she was
all the more surprised to see Harry appearing hopeful as he left behind some of
his business cards on their table and at a
couple of other spots around the lounge
as happy hour came to a close and people
started filtering away.

"I didn't expect anyone to tell me anything useful with so many other people watching," he said to her as they approached the front exit. "But there's a good chance at least one of those people will call me later."

He abruptly stopped several feet short of the front door, pulled out his phone and tapped the screen. She could hear him talking to Leon and asking him to drive over and park in a spot where he could see the front door of the Water Grill when they walked out.

"Just like there's a chance that one of those people we spoke with might help us later, there's also the possibility that one of them is friends with Darrin and didn't admit it," he explained. "They could have been texting him a warning while they were smiling at us. There are plenty of two-faced people in the world. I want Leon parked outside in case Darrin or one of his accomplices is out there waiting for us."

Ramona felt a chill pass over her skin. She glanced at Harry, grateful that he was beside her, looking out for her, and that he was good at his job.

A few minutes later, Leon sent a text letting Harry know he was in position outside.

As they left the restaurant, a light rain fell, further intensifying the chill that was lingering in Ramona's body. Her nerves were on edge every step of the way until they reached the relative safety of Harry's truck. Driving across town as they headed back toward Cassie's ranch, she looked at the town lights glowing in the evening's increasing darkness. She'd spent nearly her entire life in Stone River and had always thought of it as a safe little town inhabited by mostly decent, trustworthy people. Now, she wasn't so sure.

About the only thing she did know for certain was that Darrin Linder was a desperate man who wanted her dead. And that he had the will to make that happen.

* * *

Harry steered his truck onto the long drive to Cassie's house, watching his mirrors to see if anyone was following him as he thought about the next steps in his quest to find Linder and his henchmen.

He'd brought Ramona to the ranch an hour ago after their visit to the Water Grill. Following that, he'd made a quick trip to the house trailer he kept at his parents' ranch so he could grab some clean clothes. He was hoping and praying for a quick resolution to the capture of Darrin and his crew, but it made sense to be prepared for a longer stay at North Star Ranch, just in case.

The light rain that had begun falling while he and Ramona were at the lounge was coming down harder now, bringing a bone-deep chill with it. Sometimes when spring officially arrived on the calendar, people around Stone River, Harry included, got so excited about the upcoming warmer weather that they forgot that there could still be seriously unpleasant days ahead. Even so, he loved it here and had literally dreamed about north Idaho while he was stationed overseas.

After his last deployment was finally over, he'd been home for a little over four months when the day came that turned his life on end. Harry was at a hardware store in town on a Saturday afternoon, buying replacement parts for his grandparents' washing machine, when his phone rang. When he answered, his mom immediately asked him where he was. Her voice had sounded wrong. Shaky and hesitant.

She told him to drive straight to the hospital. Willa had collapsed while doing some chores at the family ranch and an ambulance was already on its way.

Later that night, one nightmare was over. But another one was just beginning. The damage to Willa's brain from a ruptured aneurysm was too severe. There was nothing the doctors could do to save her.

Harry couldn't help thinking that if he'd

been at the ranch with Willa instead of at the hardware store, things might have been different. She might still be alive.

His family and friends repeatedly told him he was wrong. That when she'd collapsed while cleaning out the tack room in the stables, one of the ranch hands had seen it happen and called 9-1-1 right away. Everything that could have been done had been done.

Sometimes, when he was beating himself up for not being there, for not saving his wife's life, Bible verses reminding him that God was ultimately in control would come to mind. But knowing that did not let Harry off the hook. He had a responsibility to protect his wife, and he'd failed.

He took a deep breath and focused on the driveway in front of him. Up ahead, he saw the warm lights from the sprawling house at North Star Ranch spilling out through the windows. His heartbeat sped up and he felt a little anxious. In a good way. Truth was, he was looking forward to seeing Ramona.

Willa had been gone for four years now. He'd finally taken off his wedding band a year after she passed away but it hadn't changed how he felt—still married, still committed.

But now he'd met Ramona and things felt *different*. Like some part of his heart that had been lying dormant was beginning to stir to life. It was strange because he barely knew her. Not to mention he'd met her under the worst possible circumstances. Besides, she was scared and vulnerable right now. He needed to respect that.

He parked his truck and walked up to the front of the house, the frantic barking of Adam's dogs greeting him before he even opened the door. Since Duke was almost the size of a pony, Harry barely had to lean over to pet him as he walked through the door. Tinker, on the other hand, wasn't even tall enough to reach the top of Harry's cowboy boots, so Harry had to squat down to pet him. He didn't want the little dandelion-puff guy to feel left out.

"Dinner's almost ready," Adam called out. A savory-smelling roast was steaming in a pan on the countertop.

The front of the house was basically one giant great room, and Sherry called out a greeting from the dining area while she set the table. After exchanging a few words with both of them, Harry headed back toward the spare bedroom he was using to drop off the daypack holding his clothes. He was halfway down the hallway when Ramona stepped out of the home office and beckoned to him.

"What's up?" Harry asked, keeping his tone businesslike.

Ramona held up her phone. "I got a text from Jasmine. She thought of something that might help us track Darrin, but she said it would be easier to explain in an actual call. And she wants to talk to both of us."

Harry snapped his wandering thoughts and feelings back under control in an instant. Until Darrin was locked up, Ramona would not be safe. Nothing was more important than that. "Okay," he said. "Let's call her."

They walked into the office and Harry dropped his daypack into a chair. Ramona set her phone on one of the desks and made the call, putting it on speaker.

Jasmine answered right away. "Hey, are both of you guys there?" she asked.

"Yes," Harry and Ramona answered in unison.

"Okay, so I didn't even think of this until just before I texted Ramona, and maybe it's nothing, but I wanted to tell you that I went with Darrin up to Bridger on a ski trip once. Maybe that's where he's hiding out."

"At one of the ski resorts?" Harry asked, grabbing a pen from the desktop.

He pulled a blank sheet of paper out of a printer tray. "Which one?"

"Not one of the resorts," she said. "He's got a small house in town."

"A time-share?" Harry asked. If it was a time-share, it could be occupied by someone else right now, making it an unlikely hideout.

"No, nothing like that. It's just a little vacation house, one of those prefab things. It's owned by some friends of Darrin's parents. They let Darrin, his parents and some of their other friends use it whenever they want to head over to Idaho to ski in the winter or swim in one of the nearby lakes in summer."

Okay, so it sounded like the house was empty a lot of the time. And it wasn't in Darrin's name, so there was no paperwork to tie it to him. That would make it a good hideout. "What's the address?" Harry asked, pen poised over the paper.

"I don't know." Jasmine blew out a puff of air that made it sound like she was frustrated with herself. "Ever since I thought of the ski trip, I've been trying to remember some of the landmarks on the way there. I mean, obviously you drive up to Bridger to start, but I'm trying to remember which way you go from there. I've looked at some online maps but they're just confusing me. If you want to go up there, I can try to draw a map for you from memory. It won't be exact, but I'll do the best I can."

Ramona made eye contact with Harry and he nodded.

"Okay, we'll go check it out," Ramona said. "Shall we come by your office in the morning to talk to you and get your map?"

"Come by the condo. I'm going into the office a couple of hours late. Alex is finally coming by to install that security system."

"Okay, we'll see you about eight," Ramona said before disconnecting the call.

Sherry stepped into the office to let them know dinner was ready.

After he sat down, Harry glanced around the dining table. Everyone sitting down to eat together made it look as if life was going along like normal, but he knew it wasn't. He felt uneasy about Jasmine's sudden memory of the house near the ski resorts.

Right now, she was the best source of information he had. But he still wasn't sure how much he could trust her, or how easily she could be manipulated by people with evil intentions.

SEVEN

The living room at Jasmine's condo felt crowded the following morning.

"Harry, this is Alex Ferrano," Jasmine said, making the introductions between the bounty hunter and the builder of the condo development. Ramona had already met Alex. He'd been to the condo several times back when Ramona still lived there to make the repairs and take care of all the usual "new building" problems. He was a young, ambitious man who worked hard.

Ramona watched the two men shake hands. Alex glanced in her direction, smiled and nodded. "Good to see you again, Ramona." Then his smiled faltered. "But it's a shame about the circumstances."

Indeed. Needing a security system for protection against a violent man who'd lost all reason was definitely a sad circumstance. But Ramona simply nodded in return and said, "Good to see you, too."

The two technicians Alex had brought with him were already wandering throughout the condo, checking for the best spots to place cameras and a couple of backup control panels in case Jasmine ever needed to access her system and her phone wasn't handy.

There was one more person in the living room. Sitting in a club chair, fidgeting and restless, was a man who appeared to be in his late twenties. He looked like he'd rather be anywhere other than here. That had to be the guy Jasmine had texted Ramona about last night, Caleb Petrov.

The text had come a couple of hours after Ramona finished eating dinner and helping clean up the kitchen. Jasmine had been contacted by a friend of a friend who happened to be at the Water Grill lounge while Ramona and Harry were there. He had information about Darrin that he thought might be helpful.

But Caleb hadn't wanted to call Harry directly. He said he was worried that the bounty hunter might record the conversation.

Jasmine waited until Alex and his workers went back to their trucks to start gathering equipment before she introduced Caleb to Ramona and Harry. Even then, Caleb spoke in low tones. His gazed darted nervously between the three people in the room and the front door, giving Ramona the impression that he wanted to get out of there as fast as he could.

"What do you have to tell me?" Harry asked.

Caleb, dressed in a suit and a white shirt, tugged at his tie a couple of times and then smoothed it against his chest before finally speaking. "I sell real estate. Residential and commercial. Darrin Linder came to me about six weeks ago looking for a specific kind of property. He wanted something on Lake Bell, in one of the secluded coves on the backside of the lake where there aren't many people." Caleb took a deep breath, blew it out and finally stopped fidgeting with his tie. "He wanted something with a private pier or a dock. He also wanted the property to have a barn or a large storage shed."

"Sounds like he wants a place where he can distribute his drugs and guns or whatever else he's dealing without anyone noticing him," Jasmine said quietly. "I've been to a house in one of those coves that's only accessible by boat. It would be hard for the police or anyone else to sneak up on a person. That sounds exactly like something Darrin would want."

Harry nodded. "Okay. Did he buy anything?"

"No, not from me. I started doing some

research to find what he was looking for, but when I tried to contact him to show him some of the properties, he took forever to get back to me. When he finally did get in touch, he told me he was no longer interested and that I needed to keep my mouth shut about the whole thing."

"You think he found what he was looking for and bought it from someone else?" Harry asked.

"Maybe. Before I came over here this morning, I did a quick search on recent property purchases on Lake Bell, but nothing came up connected to his name."

"He might have had someone else pretend to be the buyer," Ramona suggested.

Caleb nodded in agreement. "Or he might have thought he could keep the transaction quiet if he bought directly from the seller rather than going through a realtor. Also, eight weeks isn't much time when you're talking about a real estate transaction. Title searches and all the other details that need to be taken care of take time. So, maybe the sale is pending. Or maybe somebody is renting to him instead."

"Why did you want to tell me about this instead of the cops?" Harry asked.

Caleb sat back in his chair and ran his hands through his hair. When he was focused on real estate, he'd calmed down a little, but now he looked uncomfortable again.

"When Darrin first contacted me, I had no idea who he was," he said. "But he seemed edgy and his emphasis on secrecy had me concerned. It was a weird experience all the way around. So, I was talking about it with my family one Sunday when I went to my parents' house for dinner, and I saw my youngest brother starting to look nervous."

Caleb sighed heavily before continuing. "My brother told me later that he knew some people who'd bought drugs from Darrin." He shook his head. "I wasn't sure what I should do in a situation like this. I didn't want to go to the cops and possibly get my brother's friends in trouble. And honestly, right now my main concern is that my brother might be using drugs, too." His voice cracked. "He's only eighteen, still at that age where he thinks he's invincible and takes stupid risks."

He took a minute to breathe deep and compose himself. "Also, I was afraid if I gave information to the cops and Darrin heard about it, he'd take out his rage on my brother." Caleb looked at Harry. "I was trying to figure out the best thing to do. So, when you showed up at the lounge, I felt like talking to you was my answer."

"You want to help Darrin get locked up, but you want to keep your name and your brother's name out of it?" Harry asked.

"Exactly. My brother's heard things that make me worry about how much damage Darrin could do. He says Darrin has expanded into weapon sales. He's formed a network of people who buy guns at gun shows—or steal them—and he resells them to people who could never buy them legally. Mostly criminal gangs out of Seattle or Portland or Los Angeles. It's turning out to be a pretty lucrative business."

"So right now, Linder's got a lot of motivation to stay near Stone River," Harry said. "It's unlikely he'd flee the area for any length of time and risk losing his connections and his business. It would take time for him to reestablish that someplace else."

Caleb got to his feet as did Ramona and Harry. Caleb slid his phone out of his pocket. "I didn't pick up one of your cards at the lounge last night because I was afraid someone would see me and word would get to Darrin. But if you want to give me your contact information, I'll use the resources I have to look for properties Darrin might be using."

Harry rattled off his phone number and email address.

Caleb tapped the information into his

phone. "I've got to head in to work. But I'll be in touch."

Harry walked with Caleb to the door and followed him outside a few steps. Ramona moved toward the front window, where she could see both men looking up and down the street. Finally, Caleb headed toward a car parked at the curb, climbed inside and drove off.

A little farther down the street, Alex and his workers stood outside a panel van. One of the workers held a power drill while the other picked up some cardboard boxes that looked like they might hold security equipment for the installation. Alex held an electronic tablet in one hand and a box in the other. All three of them started heading toward Jasmine's front door.

Harry stepped back inside. "We should probably get going," he said to Ramona.

Ramona glanced at a folded sheet of paper in her hand. Jasmine had printed out a map of the small town of Bridger, highlighting a couple possible turns inside town that might take them to the right house. When they found a house that fit Jasmine's general description, they were supposed to text her a photo and she'd tell them if it was the right place.

Jasmine had also promised to call Paul Robel, owner of the Nature Zone Sports Shoppe in Bridger, and ask if he'd be available to speak with Ramona and Harry when they arrived in a couple of hours.

Darrin had introduced Jasmine to Paul when the three of them had crossed paths at a restaurant in Bridger. The two men were obviously acquaintances, but they didn't appear to be especially close friends. The hope was that Jasmine's endorsement of Ramona and Harry's visit might encourage Paul to answer their questions about whether or not Darrin had been in town recently. And maybe he would offer suggestions of any other places around Bridger where Darrin might be hiding.

"I got another text from Darrin," Jasmine said quietly just before Ramona and Harry stepped out the door.

They both turned to look at her.

"I didn't want to talk about it in front of Caleb," she added quickly. "And before you ask, yes, I let Sergeant Bergman know."

"What did the text say?" Harry asked.

Jasmine picked up her phone from the coffee table, tapped the screen a couple of times and then read aloud, "I know now we are meant to be together. Life is empty without you. Others are trying to come between us. I will stop them. For good."

The memory of being chased through the dark woods—and shot at—flashed through Ramona's mind. He knees weakened and she quickly grabbed the back of a chair to hold herself steady. She was one of *the others* Darrin was referring to when he said he'd stop them for good.

Or maybe the term really referred to her alone.

Either way, she was certain that in his twisted mind he still saw Ramona as the main obstacle on the path to his reunion with Jasmine and the stumbling to his future happiness. And he was still intent on killing her.

"Sorry, but I can't help you." The owner of the Nature Zone Sports Shoppe leaned back against one of the counters in his store and crossed his arms over his chest.

Harry looked at him a little more closely. Paul Robel was a slender man with sun-streaked blond hair that reached his shoulders, and he moved with the easy grace of a younger man. You had to get up close to realize he was fifty years old if he was a day.

"I only know Darrin Linder because he comes into the shop a couple of times a year, typically once during ski season and then once again over the summer,"

Paul continued. "I run into him every now and then in town or on the ski slope. But that's it." He shook his head. "Man, I didn't even know he was in trouble with the police until his girlfriend called."

"*Ex*-girlfriend," Ramona said.

Harry glanced over at her before he continued questioning the store owner. "Do you have any record of his address for deliveries, maybe? We're looking for the address of the house where he stays here in town."

Paul retreated to the back office and came back a few minutes later. "Sorry, I don't have any kind of account information for him at all."

"Any thoughts on where he might go if he wanted to hide around here? Could you tell me the places he likes to hang out when he's in town? Maybe give me the names of some local friends?"

"I have no idea about any of that," Paul said stiffly. He looked toward the line of customers waiting to be rung up by the sole cashier, then turned back to Ramona and Harry. "Like I said, sorry I can't help you. But right now, I need to get back to work. This end-of-season sale for winter equipment will be my last big hurrah until June. Sales will be slow until then."

"Of course," Harry said, handing him a business card. "And please call me if you think of anything."

He and Ramona walked out to his truck. He called Cassie to give her a quick update as they started driving through town, using Jasmine's map as a general guide. The first two streets she'd indicated as possibilities didn't have any houses that looked like the one she described. But the third street did have a house that appeared to be a likely candidate. By then, Harry had already ended his phone call with Cassie.

He and Ramona sat in the truck, engine idling, while Ramona snapped a quick picture of the house and sent it to Jasmine. Within a couple of minutes, her phone rang. It was Jasmine, confirming that this was the house she'd been to with Darrin.

"It doesn't look like anyone's home right now," Harry said as soon as Ramona disconnected her call.

Even though it was midday, heavy cloud cover shaded the small town. Most of the buildings had some kind of electrical lighting visible through the windows. The dark green single-story house they were parked in front of did not.

Harry gestured at the narrow drive that ran beside the house to a building toward the back. "They got snow a few days ago, and there are tire tracks heading toward what I'm guessing is a garage," he said. "Someone's been here recently."

"This is used by several people as a vacation house," Ramona reminded him. "The tracks could be from the owner or one of the vacationers. Or maybe even a caretaker."

"Maybe," Harry said. But he was looking at the snow on the front walkway, the steps leading up to the front porch and the porch itself. It seemed reasonable that anyone staying there would clear those off. But maybe they wouldn't if they didn't want anyone to know they were there.

He sent a quick text to Cassie with the address and a request for her to find as much information about the residence as she could.

"What's your plan?" Ramona asked.

"Well, I'm not going to leave you alone in the truck, so you're coming with me. And I want you to stay behind me. I'm going to walk up to the front door and knock. If nobody answers, we'll walk around a little bit to see what we can see." He turned to her. "And if there's trouble, I want you to run and hide and call 9-1-1."

She looked at him and nodded solemnly.

They walked up to the porch of the house, and Harry knocked on the front door. He gave it a minute, and when there was no response, he knocked again. After that he rang the doorbell a few times, knocked again, and then called out, "Hello! Is anybody in the house?"

He listened for the sound of someone inside walking around, talking, whispering, anything.

The only noise he could hear came from the neighborhood around them. He took a couple of steps back and looked to each end of the house in the off chance that someone might try to run past him and make an escape. But he didn't see anybody.

"Should we look in all the windows now?" Ramona asked. "And what if someone is in there and they call the cops on us?"

Now that she looked earnest instead of solemn, Harry found himself smiling a little. She was such an intriguing combination of logic and eccentricity in the way she thought about things. It made her fun to be around. Even in a serious situation. "If someone calls the police, we'll simply explain ourselves," he said. "Everything will be fine."

He tried to look into the window by the front door, but the curtains covering them had a thick lining and he couldn't see through them. Then he made his way through the snow to each of the house's windows, grateful that he wasn't trying to do this in the dead of winter when the snow could easily be chest-high on him and almost above Ramona's head.

He was able to see through curtain gaps in a couple of windows, but the dreary day and lack of lighting inside made it impossible for him to see anything other than vague outlines. None of the outlines looked like people, nor did they move, so by the time he got to the kitchen window he was pretty convinced there was no one inside.

In the kitchen, a small wall light illuminated the interior fairly well.

"What can you see?" Ramona asked.

Since she was several inches shorter than Harry, she didn't have the clear view that he had. "There's nothing sitting on the countertops or on the table," he said, still peering into the window. "No food containers or cups or dirty dishes." He stepped back from the window. "It doesn't look like anyone's been in there recently."

Ramona sighed. "Well, it was just an idea Jasmine had. She didn't have reason to think he was out here. She just figured it would make a good hiding place."

"In this line of work, it's common to check out a whole lot of places where your bail jumper *isn't* before you find the place where he actually *is*," Harry said. "But before we write this place off, let's go check out the garage."

There was a large metal roll-up door at the front of the wooden outbuilding. It was closed and padlocked, but there were indeed tire tracks in the patches of snow in the drive leading up to it. The garage, which had a high, pitched roof, was weathered-looking and appeared to have been a do-it-yourself project completed on a modest budget. There was a narrow skylight high on the east side, apparently to capture daylight while keeping the building relatively secure. There was a standard door on the south side.

That side door was open. Not hanging open, exactly, but the latch wasn't clicked into place and there was no padlock on it to keep it closed. Harry started walking toward it.

"Should we open it and take a look?" Ramona said. Obviously, she was focusing on the same thing Harry had just noticed.

Harry reached for the handle and pulled the door open. Faint daylight fell into the interior just a few feet past the doorway. He listened for a moment, his heartbeat speeding up, his hand hovering near his holster. Then he stretched his hand toward the wall to his right, found a light switch and flicked it. A weak overhead light blinked on.

There was a lot of stuff crammed inside the building. None of it looked particularly valuable. No tools. No expensive ski equipment. Just junk, like a large pile of scrap lumber near the door and some stacks of newspaper, probably used for starting fires in the fireplace in the house. There were some trash cans and a crusty-looking grill that made the closed-up building smell like lighter fluid.

In the center of the building there was a row of old bookcases holding some basic yard equipment, some tire chains and a few other items. Sheets of plywood were propped up against the bookcases along with some plastic tarps.

Harry wanted to see what was on the other side of the garage, the side that lined up directly with the tire tracks he'd seen in the driveway. Maybe Darrin *had* come to Bridger to hide out. Maybe he wasn't using this actual house, but he could be using the garage to hide his vehicle so he could lie low somewhere in town.

Harry walked around the bookcases and tarps, with Ramona right on his heels. He was disappointed to see there was no vehicle parked there.

A sudden sound alerted him that the side door had opened wider, and he spun around, shoving Ramona behind him. Something glass was flung into the room and it broke against the floor on the other side of the bookcases. He heard a whoosh, smelled gasoline and felt a wave of heat from open flames.

He ran around the shelves and sprinted toward the door, but it was slammed shut from the outside before he could reach it. And then he heard a padlock being shoved into place on the outside latch, locking them in.

Meanwhile, the pile of newspapers and scrap lumber were ablaze, the flames already licking the walls of the garage and starting to reach toward the wooden beams overhead.

The place reeked of gasoline.

The smell of lighter fluid that he'd assumed came from the grill was actually all around the inside of the building, on all the surfaces. Someone had filled a glass bottle with gasoline, stuffed a rag in the neck, then set the rag on fire and thrown it into the soaked garage. The perfect fire-starter.

Harry tried to force the side door open, but it wouldn't budge.

The smoke was already getting thick inside the buttoned-up building and it was getting hot.

He looked around for something, anything, he could use as a tool to help them escape.

And then the overhead light went out. The thickening smoke dimmed the glow of the fire, making it hard for him to see much of anything.

"Harry?" Ramona came up beside him,

grabbed hold of his hand and squeezed it tight. Harry squeezed back.

Someone had set up an elaborate trap. And they'd walked right into it.

EIGHT

"**P**lease hurry!" Ramona shouted into her phone. Between the sounds of burning wood cracking and popping and Harry dragging things around inside the garage, it was hard for her to hear the 9-1-1 operator.

"I need a hand over here," Harry called out. He was dragging bookcases and other large items she couldn't quite make out over toward the skylight. Her guess was that he was stacking them up so he could climb up to break through the glass and escape.

Ramona's lungs were burning from the smoke and she started coughing, each spasm making her lungs feel like someone was rubbing sandpaper against them.

She could feel the pressure of an asthma attack building, but she'd left her inhaler in her purse and that was back in Harry's truck.

"Fire and EMS crews have already been dispatched," the operator said calmly. "I need you to stay on the line with me in case they need further directions when they arrive on scene."

"Ramona!" Harry's call to her had an even greater punch of urgency to it this time.

"Remind responders that we're trapped in the garage *behind* the house," Ramona said into the phone. "That's where the fire is. I've got to go."

She kept the call connected but switched the phone to speaker mode and shoved it into her pocket. The smoke was getting unbearably thick, and the heat rolling off the flames had her feeling dizzy and nauseated.

Wheezing and coughing, she stumbled toward Harry. He'd found an old, oversize, steel ice chest and shoved it against the wall below the skylight. Then he'd tipped over the tallest bookcase to dump everything off of it, dragged it over and put it on top of the ice chest. But the uppermost shelf reached a point at least four feet below the bottom edge of the skylight.

Harry reached out to her, both of his big hands clasping her upper arms. He leaned down so that his face was close to hers and she could see a reflection of the flickering flames in his eyes. "If we get you to the top shelf, can you pull yourself up and out through the skylight?"

She pulled her right arm free from his grip to cover her mouth while another coughing fit hit her. Each cough meant she drew in another lungful of smoky air and the wheezing grew stronger.

She wanted to say *yes*, that she could do it. After everything he'd done for her, she didn't want to let him down. But the truth was that given how light-headed she was feeling from lack of oxygen, she wasn't sure what she'd be able to do.

"Give me a pole or a rake or something and I can climb up and use that to reach the skylight and break it," she said in answer to his question. "That will get us some fresh air in here until the fire department arrives."

And that had better be *really* soon. The fire was growing at an especially alarming rate.

"A rush of air could fuel the fire and make it more intense," Harry said, sounding calm but very focused. He finally let go of her left arm. "We're both going to climb up. You'll go first, but I'll be right behind you. And I'll help you get out the skylight."

She worried that she couldn't stay steady on her feet as she climbed the bookcase, and that she'd cause them both to fall. But what other option did she have? Fire had already reached the overhead beams. She could hear the wood cracking and moaning. The roof could collapse at any second.

Harry had her hand by the hand and started moving closer to the bookcase. Then he grabbed a long pole with a fishing net at the end. "When we get to the top, I'll use this to break the skylight and push as much glass as I can out of the way. Then we'll toss my jacket across the bottom of the frame so you don't cut yourself. And I'll boost you out the opening."

"It's going to be a long drop on the other side," she said, fighting to take in enough air to get the words out.

Just then a crossbeam overhead broke and a chunk of the wood fell, sending up a spray of glowing red embers. It was all the reminder she needed that a fall could mean broken bones—but staying put would definitely lead to her death.

"Okay," she said quickly, nodding her head. "Okay. Let's do this."

She scrabbled up the bookcase, which

didn't feel particularly steady. Harry climbed up close behind her, talking to her, calling out to tell her that she was doing a good job and to keep going. Shaky with fear and adrenaline, she finally made it to the very top.

Harry came up alongside her. He took the fishing net, turned the handle end toward the window and punched through the glass. A rush of cool air blasted in and the flames behind them flared brighter, eagerly eating up the new source of oxygen. He pushed the pole around a few more times to clear away glass.

Then he dropped the pole, took off his jacket and flung it up toward the windowsill. Before she could say anything, he knelt down, wrapped his arms around her shins and started to lift her up. She bent over and at first, she balanced her free hand on his shoulder to hold herself steady. As he lifted her higher, she straightened up and then reached for the sides of the skylight.

She took a deep gulp of fresh air and looked out. And then she looked down. It was a long way to the ground, but at least there was some snow piled up against the side of the building. And something else, snow-covered, but with an irregular outline. Something that might help to break her fall. She couldn't identify it—and didn't have the time to think about it for long. She was holding up Harry's escape and she needed to get moving.

Dear Lord, please help us, she prayed. And then she jumped.

She landed on her left hip, falling a couple of feet into the snow where she hit something more solid. She bounced a little and then rolled until she came to a stop.

Stunned, she lay still for a moment until Harry called out the window, "Are you all right?"

She moved each of her limbs a little and it didn't feel like anything was broken. But she'd had the wind knocked out of her and couldn't quite catch her breath to reply, so she just raised a hand and waved.

She heard something crashing inside the garage. It sounded like part of the roof. And then Harry jumped out of the window, landing in the snow, sliding and rolling until he came to a stop. Unlike Ramona, he quickly got to his feet. He hurried over to her.

"I'm okay," she wheezed as he helped her sit up.

Something else crashed inside the garage as the west-facing wall collapsed inward.

Harry got her to her feet and practically carried her away from the building, now fully engulfed in flames. She could hear sirens. It sounded like a fire engine was coming up the drive. Red lights flashed across the side of the house and on the nearby snow.

Harry wrapped his arms around her and she collapsed into him, soaking up the strength and warmth and comfort he offered. How could it be true that she'd only met this man days ago when it felt like they'd been together for a long time? And that they belonged together.

She heard voices and the sounds of emergency personnel talking over radios.

Then she heard a sharp popping sound. And another. Snow kicked up at the feet. And then the bark on a nearby tree splintered.

Harry pushed her to the ground, shielding her body with his.

Those weren't popping sounds. They were sounds of rifle fire. Somebody was *shooting* at them.

"Captain Hyatt from Bridger PD let us know that one of her officers found a couple of shell casings about twenty yards from where you stood," Sergeant Bergman said. "I don't know how the shooter missed hitting you from that close of a distance. My guess is that they were trying to shoot and run away at the same time."

Five hours had passed since Ramona and Harry had walked into that garage and nearly lost their lives. The building had been a total loss, collapsing completely as soon as the firefighters started hitting it with heavy streams of water. An EMT on scene had convinced Ramona to go to the town's small hospital to treat her asthma and get checked out by a physician. She'd had Harry drive her rather than riding in an ambulance. A couple of hits from her inhaler had helped a lot, but Harry had insisted she go anyway.

After that, they talked to the local police about everything that had happened. Captain Hyatt had ordered them a pizza to eat while they were at the station. Ramona had been surprised to find herself ravenous when it arrived. She would have expected to have the whole experience kill her appetite, but it hadn't. Maybe it had something to do with the fact that after this attempt on her life—on *their* lives—she was more angry than frightened. Not because she had suddenly gotten a lot braver, but because she was tired of feeling so fearful.

Right now, she was in the bail bonds office in downtown Stone River, seated on the couch in the lobby beside Harry. The police department was only a block away, and the sergeant had walked over to give them an update on the police investigation in Bridger. Cassie was there along with Leon and Martin, the third bounty hunter who worked with Harry.

"Could finding the bullet casings help you find the shooter?" Ramona asked. Her voice sounded husky and her throat was scratchy from smoke inhalation.

"Not necessarily," Bergman said. "Not unless the police in Bridger can recover fingerprints. But they're still looking to recover slugs. And if they can connect those to a registered gun, or maybe to a gun in the possession of someone we're able to arrest, that would help with an eventual conviction."

Beside her, Harry let out a sigh. "I should have known better than to just walk in there," he said. He reached over for Ramona's hand and squeezed it. "I'm sorry."

"Nobody gets things right one hundred percent of the time," Bergman said in his usual matter-of-fact tone. "You learn from the experience, determine you're not going to repeat that same mistake, and you move on."

Ramona could see by the tight expression on Harry's face that the cop's comment hadn't sunk in at all. No surprise. Harry's frustration with himself had been evident on the two-hour drive home. It wasn't just injured pride or bruised ego. He really seemed to think it was his responsibility to do everything perfectly.

"What about Paul?" Harry asked Bergman. "The guy at the sports shop? I told the cops in Bridger that we talked with him. He could have warned Linder we were poking around. Have they found any evidence that he was involved?"

She and Harry had discussed the question of who could have known they were headed up to Bridger to check on the vacation house. Paul was one obvious possibility. And much as Ramona hated to admit it, the other obvious possibility was Jasmine. Ramona held on to the hope that even if Jasmine was the source, that the giveaway might have been inadvertent. Maybe she'd somehow accidentally spilled the beans, mentioned something to someone she thought she could trust and that person had passed the word along.

Ramona had called her cousin when she and Harry got back to town. She'd left a message telling Jasmine that they were at the bail bonds office and that she needed to talk to her. So far, she hadn't heard back.

Darrin *had* to somehow be connected to the trap and the fire in the garage. Maybe he'd been there himself. Or maybe he'd had someone else set it up.

"Paul is a high-profile citizen in Bridger," the sergeant said. "He's owned that shop for a long time. He sponsors several kids' sports teams in town. Donates to some civic charities."

"Some of the smartest criminals embed themselves in the community so they can hide in plain sight," Harry said. "Do all the right things so they look like nice people no one would suspect."

"Sadly, that's true," Bergman said. "They're checking him out, but they're keeping it low profile for now."

"What about the police here in Stone River?" Ramona asked. "Have you gotten any leads on where Darrin's been hiding out or on the identities of the other two creeps working with him?"

"I can only tell you that we have *not* identified the two accomplices. And as far as we know, Darrin Linder could be anywhere."

Ramona blew out a sigh and shifted her weight on the sofa. Her lungs were feeling better, but now her hip and shoulder were sore from where she'd landed on them. In all likelihood, they were going to feel even worse tomorrow. But she was alive. And things could have gone much worse.

Thank You, Lord, Ramona prayed silently. She tried to catch Harry's eye to offer him a reassuring smile, but he was staring down at his boots. She wanted him to know that rather than blame him for what had happened, she appreciated him for doing everything he could to keep her safe. And that included risking his own life. More than once. His job was to track and recover bail jumper Darrin Linder. No one was paying him to keep her safe. But he'd gone far beyond what anyone could have expected from him because he was a good person.

Ramona glanced around at Cassie, Leon and Martin. They were all good people, willing to do whatever they could to help her. She was determined to focus on that, rather than on her fear that Darrin would eventually kill her.

Bergman stayed for a few more minutes and then headed back to the police station.

"What did you two learn from your visit over to the coast to talk to Darrin's parents?" Harry asked Leon and Martin.

Both men walked over from where they were leaning against their desks and dropped into the chairs across from the sofa. Cassie was still seated at her desk, but she turned away slightly to speak on the phone with someone.

"Darrin's parents said they were worried about him and I believe them," Martin said.

Martin Silverdeer looked to be a little bit younger than Harry and Leon, with black hair and very dark brown eyes, dusky skin and aquiline features.

"They said Darrin had changed a lot

over the last couple of months," Martin continued. "They tried to talk to him about it but he blew them off. And then, after he got arrested and they found out he was dealing drugs, they started trying to get an intervention organized. But he jumped bail and disappeared before they could make that happen."

"They said they hadn't seen him or heard from him since he got out of jail, but that they'd call us if he did contact them," Leon added. "His dad said they'd rather have him locked up and angry with them than have him hurting someone or dead."

"What about Jasmine?" Harry turned to Ramona. "You still haven't heard back from her?"

Ramona reached for her purse on the ground near her feet to grab her phone. She sucked in a breath to keep herself from yelping in pain. She wasn't aware of how stiff she was until she tried to move. Now it felt like every muscle in her body was strained and sore. Maybe it was from the fall out the window. Or maybe it was because she'd had to use muscles she barely knew she had to climb up the stupid bookcase when she was fighting to make her escape from the smoke and flames. Or it could be from running for her life—twice. Or the lack of sleep since this whole thing began.

Come to think of it, she was pretty amazed she could still walk at all.

She tapped the screen of her phone as she sat back up and saw that she'd received a text from her cousin. Will meet you at the bail bond office as soon as I get off of work. She read it aloud and then glanced at a wall clock. "She should have gotten off work fifteen minutes ago, so I expect she'll be here any minute."

Harry turned to her. "All right, why don't you just sit here and rest while we're waiting for her to show up? I'm going to brew some coffee and take a look at my email. I've got some other cases I'm working, and I need to check for updated information anyone's sent me."

"Of course," Ramona said, much more chipper than she genuinely felt. Partly because she liked sitting close to him and didn't want him to leave. And partly because his reference to his other cases was a reminder that the working relationship, or working friendship, or *whatever* it was they had, was a temporary deal. It might mean a lot to her, but it was just another day in the office for him.

It was probably a good thing that his behavior reminded her of that. The truth was that their friendship wasn't going anywhere. It was a dead-end relationship. From the way he spoke of his day-to-day life, she could tell he was still processing his wife's passing. As long as that was the case, he was not emotionally available to Ramona or any other woman. Not even if he thought he wanted to be. And she'd promised herself that she was never going to let herself be drawn into a complicated, high-drama relationship ever again.

Harry got up and walked away. The absence of his body heat beside her suddenly made her feel colder. She crossed her arms over her chest and closed her eyes. She felt tired, too. No wonder. Having an enraged criminal like Darrin Linder, and whoever he had working for him, repeatedly trying to kill you could take a lot out of a girl. She blew out a sigh.

"Hey."

Ramona opened her eyes to see Cassie standing in front of her with a folded-up plush throw in her hands. She tossed it the short distance between them and Ramona caught it.

"Thanks."

"You sure you're okay?" Cassie asked, concern etching her face.

Ramona wasn't exactly okay. She was tired and scared and sore. But Cassie and the bounty hunters were already doing everything they could to help her. So, Ramona just nodded and said, "I'm good. Thanks."

Cassie gave her a disbelieving look, then turned and walked back to her desk. Leon and Martin were also back at their desks, working on laptops or thumbing through file folders. Cassie had told her that their workdays typically started in the evening and went well into the night. And Harry had just reminded Ramona that hers was not the only case they had.

Ramona unfurled the throw over her lap and legs and leaned back into the couch, determined to leave everyone alone and let them get their work done. But then she caught a whiff of the rich aroma of coffee brewing and knew she had to have some.

When she figured enough time had passed for it to finish brewing, she tossed aside the throw and was about to stand up when the door flung open and Jasmine walked in.

"I heard what happened. I'm so glad

you're all right!" Jasmine called out, making a beeline for her cousin. She was dressed to the nines, as usual, in a stylish gray suit and narrow-heeled pumps.

Ramona groaned a little as she stood up, fighting against the soreness that was really settling into her body now, and Jasmine grabbed her in a tight hug.

"I'm so sorry all of this is happening to you," Jasmine said, teary-eyed as she finally released her embrace, but she continued to hold Ramona at arm's length, appearing to scan her for injuries.

"Stop blaming yourself. You couldn't have known all of this would happen when you started dating Darrin," Ramona said.

However, speaking of things people could or couldn't know, she found herself revisiting the question she Harry had been discussing on and off all day. How had the attacker at the garage known that Harry and Ramona were coming and when they would be there?

Looking at Jasmine right now, wiping away a tear, her big hazel eyes filled with concern, Ramona couldn't believe that her cousin could have had any connection with today's attack, or any connection at all with Darrin anymore.

Fatigue was rapidly setting in, and Ramona's thoughts and feelings seemed to tumble over one another in a random pattern. Right now, she wasn't sure of much of anything. She just knew that she needed to let her cousin know that she loved her and she was proud of her for working so hard to get her life straightened out.

Before she could speak, Harry stepped up. "Good to see you again, Jasmine." He quickly introduced the others in the office, and then gestured toward the sofa beside Ramona. "Could I talk to you for a minute?"

"Sure." Jasmine perched on the couch and Ramona sat back down beside her.

Harry sat across from them. "So, we're

trying to figure out how the bad guys knew we'd be at that house in Bridger. Do you have any ideas on that?"

Well, that was direct. Ramona could feel her cousin's posture stiffen beside her and she turned slightly so she could see her better.

"What are you saying?" Jasmine asked tightly.

"Not saying anything," Harry replied easily. He leaned back, relaxed, looking as unintimidating as possible for a man his size. "I'm just asking if you mentioned to anyone where we were going."

"I told my mom. I promised I'd keep her updated on everything."

"Did you tell her in person?"

Jasmine shook her head. "No, I told her over the phone."

"Where were you when you talked to her? Could someone else have heard the conversation?"

"I was home and there was no one else around," Jasmine said firmly. "The workers putting in the security system had left by then."

Ramona was watching her cousin closely and thought she saw a flicker of uncertainty pass over her face.

Jasmine got to her feet. "I've got to get going or I'll be late for my group therapy meeting. Believe it or not, I am committed to doing everything I can to stay sober and drug-free now." Anger flattened the line of her mouth and her brows were drawn together. "I can guess what you are thinking. That I've gone back to my old ways. But I haven't." Without waiting for a response, she quickly walked to the door, yanked it open, and left.

Ramona felt a twinge of guilt in the pit of her stomach. At the same time, she was frustrated. Changing the subject when the topic was uncomfortable was a common old-Jasmine tactic. So were the temper tantrum and the dramatic exit. It was amazing how someone could look so put together, and yet be such a mess inside.

Like Darrin Linder.

Harry moved so that he was back sitting beside Ramona. Once again, he reached for her hand. It seemed to be becoming a habit, and she liked it more than she should. "I'm sorry I upset your cousin," he said. "But not sorry enough to stop asking her hard questions."

Ramona sighed. "Backing off when things get tough is rarely the right answer."

Harry turned to her and a smiled crossed his face.

"What?" she asked.

"I'm just glad to hear you say that, considering all that's happened to you today. Considering all that's happened since Darrin came into your life, really." His smile began to fade, yet the warmth still shone in his eyes. Ramona felt drawn to it, even if an alarm seemed to sound from the depths of her heart. *Don't let yourself fall for him. He's not available for a real relationship. And there's nothing you can do to change that.*

A knot formed in her stomach as she thought about how easily she'd grown used to being around him. And about how much she liked him.

That *like* feeling was on the verge of turning into something deeper and she could not let that happen.

Her concern must have shown on her face, because Harry started looking at her more closely, his own expression more serious. "Don't worry," he said. "We'll capture Darrin. And in the meantime, I'll be right beside you to protect you from anything he tries to throw at you."

Yes, staying alive was her biggest concern. By far. Darrin was determined to kill her and the attack today in Bridger proved he had a long reach. She already knew that he had people willing to help him do his dirty work, which meant she had an unknown number of people to fear.

But losing her heart to Harry, and then having to let him go was growing into a pretty big concern, too.

NINE

On Sunday morning, Harry followed Ramona out of the little white church near Cassie's ranch right after the service ended. He didn't make a point of walking ahead of her because he knew that Martin had the area in front of the church covered. Martin had agreed to stay out there and keep watch in case Darrin Linder or his hoodlums showed up, and in return, Cassie's dad had sat in the front pew and recorded the sermon for later viewing so Martin wouldn't miss out. So far, there'd been no indication that Darrin knew where Ramona had been staying, but why take chances?

The heels on Harry's dress cowboy boots tapped loudly on the polished old wooden floor, but there wasn't a lot he could do about it. He was a fairly big guy and treading softly had never been his strong suit.

Outside the church, dappled sunlight shone through the branches of the tall evergreens. Congregants exiting the building chatted, laughed and hugged or shook hands before parting ways and heading for their vehicles. Everyone from North Star Ranch, however, moved more cautiously, scanning the area for any signs of danger.

The fire trap on Friday had shaken up all of them. Harry and Ramona had been unnerved by how close it had come to killing them. The rest of the bounty hunter crew—including Cassie's dad, plus Jay and Sherry—were unnerved by the repeated viciousness directed toward Ramona.

It was one thing to have a bail jumper work hard to avoid capture or violently resist arrest once they were found. But the crimes against Ramona since the night at the cabin were beyond reason. And that made things not only scary, but also difficult to predict.

Even with the seemingly random acts of bail jumpers who were drug-addled or lost in the throes of alcoholism, there were patterns and ways to find them. Favorite bars. Drug dealers they routinely went to for their fix. Predictable ways they would get money, like a burglary followed by a visit to a local pawn shop.

Linder, on the other hand, was different. He didn't have a substantial criminal record that could give them clues on his associates or hideouts. He seemed to have somehow gone completely underground, because so far no one—not even the police—had spotted him anywhere. Not since the night at the cabins. And he was fixated on killing Ramona with an intensity that defied logic.

She'd finally convinced Jasmine to break up with him and the man had come *unglued.* It didn't make sense. They'd only been dating for five months, according to Jasmine. They weren't engaged, so it wasn't like Ramona had interrupted the life they were planning on building together.

The only thing Harry could figure was that Linder's behavior was related to the drugs he was selling and using and they'd messed up his thinking. Or maybe the drugs triggered some deep emotional issue. Both theories could potentially be true. Whatever the motivation, he'd quickly become a very dangerous man. And that meant everybody needed to stay on their toes. All the time.

The church parking lot was a grassy area with a few patches of exposed dirt. Martin was already out there in his truck waiting for Leon. Cassie, Adam, Sherry and Jay all piled into Jay's big SUV. Harry and Ramona headed for Harry's truck.

The turnoff from the highway onto the

private road that led to North Star Ranch was only seven miles away, but Harry still insisted on taking every precaution. That was why they'd taken three vehicles, had arrived at the church together and were leaving together, with Harry and Ramona in the center vehicle. Traveling with just Ramona and Harry in one vehicle could leave them vulnerable to an attack. On the other hand, loading up with too much security could draw attention and actually make them more vulnerable.

Harry fired up the truck's engine. He hadn't even started moving yet when Ramona asked, "Do you ever wonder if you're doing the right thing with your life?"

Harry thought about her question as he shifted gears and followed Martin's truck out onto the narrow highway. "Are you taking about career choices?" he asked. "Because, yeah, I've wondered about that at times."

"Like now?"

"With bounty hunting? No. Right now, I know it's what I'm supposed to be doing." Not only did it feel like the right thing for him, but it was also something he prayed about. Often. And despite the dangers and stress that came with the job, he did feel peace in his heart about what he did for a living.

Where was she going with this line of questioning?

Harry liked to stay a couple steps ahead of any situation he was dealing with. That was how you kept control—as much as control was possible.

The trip to Bridger, and the fire, had taken place on Friday. Yesterday, Saturday, had been a quiet day at the ranch. Ramona had wanted to help out with exercising the horses and mucking the stables, but Harry had seen that she was moving stiffly, obviously still sore. He'd quietly finessed things so that she'd stayed in the house, helping Jay with some cooking while Harry worked nearby at the dining table, researching nearby lakefront properties for sale and trying to work up leads on where Darrin might be hiding out.

Ramona had called her parents a couple times during the day. She talked about how much she missed them. How much she missed working at the diner with them. Harry had gotten a little worried that she might not want to stay at the ranch any longer, but she hadn't actually mentioned anything about moving back home.

"How do you know bounty hunting is what you're supposed to be doing?" Ramona asked, redirecting his thoughts back to what was on her mind right now. "How do you know you're following the path you're supposed to be on? I'm not talking about the smart-money path or the impress-people path, I'm talking about the direction you're called to according to the Lord's purpose for your life."

"I pray about it," he said. That was something he'd done a lot of after the numbness of Willa's passing began to wear away and his future had stretched out in front of him, endless and empty.

"I've prayed a lot and I haven't gotten any clear direction," Ramona said, disappointment weighing down her voice.

"I haven't gotten my answers from a loud, booming voice like something out of a movie," Harry said, smiling at the idea. There were definitely times when he would have appreciated exactly that. "I consider my options. Sometimes I ask other people for their opinions and take wise counsel into account. I look at what the Scriptures say. And then I start taking steps toward the direction I'm drawn. Sometimes I make mistakes. But that's unavoidable. I just repeat the same steps, make a course correction and try again."

Ramona didn't respond for a while and Harry wondered if his comments hadn't been helpful or if he'd said the wrong thing.

"It's just that I want a *really* clear answer because I hate making mistakes," Ramona finally said.

Harry laughed, hard, from the pit of his stomach. "I know just how you feel—but I'm afraid there's no avoiding it," he said eventually. "It's part of life." And in that moment, it struck him that the advice he was giving to her was also true for himself. Obsessively trying to avoid making mistakes was useless.

Another thought slipped into his mind. Was it possible to love again? Not *replace* Willa, but move on toward having a family of his own, the dream he'd had since he and Willa got married? Was it time for him to step out and find out? Should he take that risk?

Fear, cold and hard, squeezed his lungs. In an instant, it felt as if he were back at the hospital in town, hearing the emergency room doctor telling him Willa was gone. He thought of the jumble of dark, desolate emotions that had tumbled through his mind for months in the aftermath of that terrible day.

Maybe he'd been fooling himself, saying that his fidelity to Willa was because of loyalty to her. Perhaps the true reason was that he didn't believe he'd survive going through something like that again. *No.* He could not repeat the experience of losing the woman he loved. He didn't need to step out to know that.

And now that he realized that, he needed to put some emotional distance between himself and Ramona. There was no sense in kidding himself. He had begun to feel a connection to her, a closeness that he'd allowed to grow because it was a feeling he'd missed for so long and was certain would never appear in his life again. But because he did care for Ramona, and because he could tell that she felt an attraction toward him, too, he had to pull back. He wouldn't give her the impression that there was the possibility of a future together for the two of them. Because there wasn't.

"I need to see my parents," Ramona said as they pulled up to the ranch house.

Harry wasn't surprised to hear her say that. She and her parents were obviously very close.

"I'd like help them at the diner for a little while. There's office stuff I usually take care of and they're running behind on some of it. They didn't ask for my help. Given the situation with Darrin, I know they *wouldn't* ask. But that doesn't change the fact that I'm letting them down."

"Can't they just let it go for now?" Harry asked as they walked into the house. "Or get someone else to do it?"

Ramona turned to him. "Someone is trying to murder their only child. They're barely able to take care of the basics right now. Finding and hiring new staff isn't really something they can manage."

Cassie turned to them as they walked

into the great room, and Harry explained the situation, certain that Cassie would back up his opinion that it was too risky. To his surprise, she didn't.

"You can certainly make your own decisions and you're free to come and go as you please," Cassie said to Ramona. "You'll be taking a chance, but sometimes that's a reasonable thing to do. You could take one of the old ranch trucks since the bad guys know what Harry's truck looks like—and take Martin with you. Maybe seeing your mom and dad will be a fresh reminder of what you're fighting for. And maybe that will give you more strength to do whatever you have to if something really terrible happens in the future."

Harry turned into the parking lot of Kitchen Table and slowed down to take a good look around. Ramona, who was seated beside him, and Martin were also checking the surroundings. Convinced that they hadn't been followed and that no one was waiting to jump them in the parking lot, Harry pulled up to the employee entrance at the back of the diner and parked parallel to the building with the passenger side just a couple of feet from the door.

"Thank you for doing this," Ramona said.

Harry cut the engine. The area wasn't marked as a fire lane, so he planned to leave the battered old truck parked right here. "You're welcome. But remember your promise to keep a low profile and to not let the visit drag on too long."

She nodded. "I remember."

He glanced at the dashboard clock. It was two o'clock. Ramona had told him that the lunch rush would be over around two and that the diner would be fairly quiet until people started showing up for dinner around four thirty.

By the time Harry got around the truck and over to her side, Ramona and Martin were already out and standing on the pavement.

"It's funny, but you can really miss the mundane, routine parts of your life when you don't have them anymore," Ramona said. She used a key to open the back door and then stepped inside. Harry was right behind her, with Martin following them.

The first thing Harry noticed was the thick, rubber, nonskid matting covering most of the floor. The next thing to catch his attention was the mouthwatering scent wafting through the air. Apples, cinnamon, sugar and butter. "That smells delicious," he said, feeling his stomach starting to growl.

"We're famous for our pies," Ramona said, an obvious note of pride in her voice.

"The sign outside mentioned that." Stone River was a small town, but not so small that Harry had eaten at every single restaurant. Apparently, he'd missed out on some good food by not stopping in here sooner.

He caught a flash of movement on his right side, discernible through the open shelving that was loaded with pots and pans and stacks of plates. He immediately reached for the gun holstered at his waist. But then Eric Miller appeared, rubbing his hands on his long, white chef's apron.

"Hey, sweetheart," Eric called out to his daughter.

Ramona stepped into his embrace, practically melting into it. This was what she had needed. Harry could see that now. Her family. Some familiarity. A hint of her old routine to remind her that life was worth fighting for even when hope was hard to find.

After Willa passed away, Harry had been in shock for at least a couple of weeks. It might have been longer. But after the shock, dark grief had kicked in. Sometimes it was hard for him to remember exactly how his life worked for those first few months after her death. His memories were a confusing blur.

And then, one day, Harry's dad had asked him if he'd be willing to wash his dad's truck for him. It was really muddy, but his dad claimed that he didn't have time to wash it himself. Harry had done it, even though he had to concentrate hard to think of each of the steps involved in the process.

Tracking down the right cleaners and the sponges that they usually used to wash the vehicles on the ranch plus all the other necessary supplies felt like it took forever. The whole process definitely took him much longer than it should have. And when he was finally finished, his dad asked him to wash mom's car.

Slowly, Harry had realized the power of doing something normal and routine. That it could help bring someone back into step with living after a traumatic experience shot them off on a cold and numbing trajectory.

So, yeah, bringing Ramona here, today, was the right decision. Even if he was worried that Linder or one of his accomplices was lurking nearby. Watching Ramona loosen her embrace with her dad and then reach for her mom who'd just appeared from around a corner confirmed that.

Looking at the small family as they reunited in front of him made him think of his parents and his brother and sister. Deep in his heart, he still yearned for a family of his own. It was difficult to admit that to himself because it meant accepting the idea of a family with someone other than Willa. And he didn't want to admit to that yearning, because even a little bit of hope sparked pain in his heart. He couldn't forget that hope had a painful side. Because there was always the possibility of disappointment and loss.

So which way did he want to go with his own life? He thought he'd settled on an answer to that question, yet here it was again.

The answer to the dilemma *should* be easy. He had to follow the path that made certain he never, ever again went through the pain he experienced when Willa died.

Another member of Ramona's family stepped through a doorway leading from a small office. The resemblance between the woman and Ramona's mom was impossible to miss. Ramona had told Harry that her Aunt Valerie would be here today to take a look at her parents' financials and make sure everything was correctly taken care of.

"Nice to meet you," Harry said, shaking Valerie's hand after they were introduced.

"Thank you so much for helping my niece," she responded, with a slight smile directed toward Ramona.

"Of course."

"And I know my daughter, Jasmine, appreciates your help, too," she continued.

How did Harry respond to that? After

the things he said the last time he saw Jasmine, he was sure he was far from her favorite person. And frankly, he still had some doubts about her possible connection to the attack in Bridger.

"Jasmine has made some bad decisions in life," Valerie said as if she could hear his thoughts. "She knows that as well as anybody. Sometimes it's hard to show gratitude to someone else when you're busy beating yourself up. But she'll get there one day, when Darrin is locked up and everything calms down."

"I'm glad I can help," Harry said.

"So, are you ready for me to do an inventory and order restocks?" Ramona asked, looking at her parents.

Eric smiled slyly. "Well, you know that's one of *my* least favorite tasks."

Ramona nodded. "I'll take care of it."

"Besides the perishable and nonperishable food items, you might want to check the cleaning supplies and linens," her mom added.

Ramona laughed and shook her head. Harry felt his heart lift a little.

"Oh, and check the packaging supplies for takeout orders," Eric said. "We get a lot more takeout orders than we used to."

"It's the way of the world these days, Dad," Ramona said, sounding like an amused teenager. "If you'd let me manage the diner, one of the first things I'd do would be to hire someone to develop an app for takeout orders and then I'd dedicate a couple of parking spaces for people who are just here to pick up their food."

"Oh, honey, you don't want to do that," Toni said. "I mean, the app thing might be a good idea. But managing the diner and everything that goes with that would take up all your time. There's no way you could do that and take business courses."

"Kiddo, we want you to have the opportunity to have a great career. One that pays well, that won't demand you work long hours on your feet all day." Eric nodded toward his sister-in-law. "Something like your aunt does—something that's professional, like accounting. That's the way to go."

Ramona kept a pleasant expression on her face. But Harry's bounty hunting experience had made him pretty good at reading body language. He could see the disappointment and resignation in Ramona's eyes and the slumping of her shoulders. He thought of her question about knowing when a person was on the right path—and the things she told him about the office job she'd lost. She really didn't want a life spent working in an office. She wanted to work here, in the diner. But clearly, there were concerns involved that couldn't be solved by a simple family conversation.

And it wasn't Harry's place to get involved. He had his own life decisions to figure out. He was by Ramona's side to keep her safe and work with her to capture Darrin Linder. Anything going on in her life beyond that wasn't his business.

Ramona went into the office with Valerie to get started on her inventory and ordering tasks. Toni walked out to the dining area at the front of the restaurant to take care of business there. Other employees filtered in and out of the kitchen area and Harry watched them closely. Especially if they went anywhere near the office where Ramona was working. They typically acknowledged Harry with a nervous smile or a nod, but they didn't ask him who he was or why he was there. They probably already had a pretty good idea about what was going on.

Eric insisted on making Harry a patty melt on rye bread with plenty of sharp cheddar cheese and a side of onion rings. Of course, it was delicious.

Two hours passed and Ramona finished up the reordering tasks for her parents. By the time she was ready to go, she seemed to have relaxed a little.

Her parents, on the other hand, had grown increasingly anxious. Harry could tell that they'd been putting on a brave face from the moment he and Ramona had arrived. What parent wouldn't be absolutely gutted with fear after some thug had either attacked or ordered the attack of their daughter three times?

Everyone exchanged their goodbyes, with multiple hugs and a few tears shed by Ramona's parents. Ramona seemed determined to appear confident and calm in front of them.

The world was a dangerous place. Ramona knew it as well as Harry did. Maybe that was why she didn't promise that she'd be seeing them again.

TEN

"Everybody knows that one of the goons who attacked Ramona had snake tattoos on the sides of his neck," Jasmine said irritably. "I've heard her mention it at least three times. If I knew someone who fit that description, don't you think I would have already said something?"

It was the morning after the visit to the diner, and Ramona and Harry had gone to Jasmine's condo to meet with Jasmine, Valerie and Sergeant Bergman to get updated on the current police investigation and take a look at some new suspect photos.

Ramona held back a frustrated sigh and reminded herself that Jasmine was going through a lot right now. Detoxing from drugs and alcohol. Daily sobriety meetings plus counseling sessions to help her face painful emotions that went all the way back to adolescence when her dad abandoned her and her mom. Jasmine was doing all of this while trying to keep her job. And on top of that, she had a murderous ex-boyfriend who'd already verbally and physically abused her, threatened her family and tried to kill her cousin. It was understandable she was feeling a little on edge.

Fortunately, the time Ramona had spent at her parent's diner yesterday had centered her emotions and that in turn helped her to be patient with Jasmine right now. People on the mend from rough times were not always easy to love as they fought their way back from a hellish situation. But that didn't mean you didn't still try.

Jasmine and Sergeant Bergman sat side by side on the sofa, with a small laptop opened up on the coffee table in front of them. The sergeant wanted her to look at mug shots of men who might be Bald Guy or Skinny Guy.

Ramona glanced at Harry, who stood with his arms crossed, leaning against the wall. Valerie was seated near her daughter, her hand on Jasmine's knee, patting it softly as if trying to calm her.

Valerie was dressed in a stylish dark blue suit, silk blouse and expensive leather pumps. She'd stopped by, announcing her intention to give Jasmine moral support while she answered the sergeant's questions, and then take her daughter out to lunch. After that, Valerie would head back to her office.

Looking at her aunt, Ramona couldn't help thinking of her own mom, who typically wore jeans and a T-shirt and comfortable flat shoes to work.

Somewhere, Ramona's parents had obviously gotten the idea that Valerie's life choices, at least in terms of her career, were the better ones. And yet her parents were happy and had a big circle of friends who loved them. That was no small thing. Did they not realize that?

"We don't know how recently he got those tattoos," Sergeant Bergman said calmly after giving Jasmine a minute to compose herself. "Maybe you saw him with Darrin before he got the tattoos." He gestured toward the laptop in front of them. "Just look at the pictures. Tell me if you recognize anybody."

Ramona impatiently waited for her turn. Sergeant Bergman wanted her and Harry to look at the photos also, but he wanted everyone to look at them separately so they wouldn't influence one another. She watched Jasmine's face anxiously, hoping to see a sign that she recognized at least one of the photos she was looking at.

They needed a break in this case, something to get it moving forward. There was still no sighting of Darrin, which was worrisome to Ramona for many reasons. She wanted him found and captured, of course. As all of this dragged out even longer, she worried that he'd left the area. What was there to keep him from heading back to Seattle where he could hide in the crowd for a while? Over time, with nothing new happening, Ramona's case would become a lower priority. Newer, active crimes would demand the attention of the police department. The bounty hunters would have to write off Darrin's bond. And at that point, Darrin could come back and achieve his goal of killing Ramona once she was no longer closely watched and protected.

So far there were no leads on a possible purchase of lakefront property by Darrin. The police hadn't found any connection between Darrin and Paul at the sport shop in Bridger. They'd checked out all the known addresses and workplaces for Darrin that they could find and had uncovered nothing. Likewise, the information on his bail bond application had turned out to be useless now that he was on the run and staying out of contact with his known associates.

"I don't recognize any of these men." Jasmine turned her gaze from the computer screen to Ramona. Her face was turning red and her eyes were filling with tears. "I'm sorry."

Ramona walked over to wrap her arms around her cousin and give her a hug. "It'll be okay." She hoped that was true.

As she let go of Jasmine, she couldn't help noticing how pale her cousin looked and the dark circles under her eyes. She'd lost weight and was down to not much more than skin and bones. She could tell that Jasmine's nerves were stretched thin. In her own way, she'd been crying out for help for years as she'd fought through depression after her dad abandoned her and her mom, but no one in the family had seen it. Or at least they hadn't recognized it for what it was. They'd just thought of it as *Jasmine going a little too far again* when her life had gotten troublesome.

Now, at least, she seemed to be on the right track. But it was still a long road to a balanced life and freedom from her past addictions. The sad part was that there wasn't much more anyone in the family could do for her other than be there for her and show their support. Ultimately, she was the one who had to complete the process.

Ramona's gaze drifted back to Harry, who was still leaning against the wall. He'd chosen a spot near the passage into the family room where he could be in the living room with everyone and see the front door while being only a few steps from a sightline to the back door. He was keeping an eye on things even though they had a police sergeant right there. Because that's how Harry was. Attentive. Protective. Putting his heart into the mission in front of him. Always committed to doing the right thing.

It was what she liked about him. *Really*

liked about him. Could maybe even love about him. If she let herself.

But she would *not* let herself fall in love with Harry. Because right now, at this very moment, the truth was hitting her hard that Harry was kind of in the same boat as Jasmine. Not that he had the same issues or addictions, but he had the death of his wife to work through. A big issue, indeed. And Ramona couldn't get him through it, though she really, *really* wanted to try. It was his situation to deal with on his own terms and with his own timing. And he'd made it pretty clear he wasn't ready to move on and start a new relationship.

If she were a better person, she might be happy for him and the woman he'd meet in the future when it was the right time for him to fall in love and get married. But when she thought about having to walk away from Harry, her heart ached. And the vague idea that everyone would be happy at some point in the future didn't cheer her up. Not at all.

As if he knew she was thinking about him, Harry turned to look at her. When their eyes met, she felt a sense of connection that was almost physical and her stomach did a little backflip in excitement. Apparently, it hadn't yet gotten the memo from her brain. It was going to take a more determined effort to back away from him emotionally.

The sergeant called Harry over to sit beside him and look at the mug shots on the laptop.

Ramona decided that this was a good time to put a little physical distance between herself and Harry. "I'm going to get some coffee." She stood up to walk to the kitchen. Jasmine and Valerie got up and walked with her.

"You said there was an issue with the fan over the stove, right?" Valerie said to Jasmine while pulling an attached stylus from the bottom of her phone and starting to jot notes on the screen.

"Yes."

Ramona started organizing things to brew a pot of coffee while the other two talked.

Valerie had fronted the down payment for Jasmine's condo. She was clearly aware that there was a time limit on the warranty that had been included with the condo purchase and she had mentioned more than once over the last month that she was afraid Jasmine wouldn't follow through on arranging for the necessary repairs that kept popping up.

"You know what," Valerie said. "I know Alex is very hard to get hold of right now. His properties are selling like crazy. Why don't you let me take care of this? You know I'll keep calling until I get a response."

"I can take care of it," Jasmine said wearily.

It wasn't Ramona's place to jump in

with an opinion, but she really hoped Valerie would let Jasmine take care of it. Her cousin needed a sense of accomplishment.

When the coffee finished brewing, Ramona poured cups for everyone. She put her own cup, plus cups for Harry and Sergeant Bergman, on a tray and carried it back to the living room.

"This guy looks familiar," Harry said quietly. His gaze was locked on the computer screen. "He was the one driving the SUV during the attack at the railroad underpass. He was wearing a mask then, but I saw him without it when he came to pick up the guy who had Ramona at gunpoint. He was one of the two losers at the shooting at the cabins, too."

Bergman didn't say anything in response. Probably sticking with his plan not to influence anyone until they'd all looked at the pictures.

Harry went through the rest of the photos. Three of them were apparently local career criminals that Harry knew by name, which meant he could tell the sergeant he hadn't seen them in this case connected to Darrin.

Finally, it was Ramona's turn. She took her time but was disappointed that she didn't recognize anyone. She was starting to wonder who could possibly have looked familiar to Harry. And then she came to a picture of a man with large shaved head and chillingly vacant eyes. "This is the guy with the snake tattoos," she said to the sergeant. Though he didn't have the tattoos in the picture. "Is this the same guy Harry picked out?"

"You know I can't confirm that until you've finished your review," Bergman said. "Go through the rest of them."

She kept going. No one else looked familiar, but that was okay, she told herself, because at least now they had a lead. "What's his name?" she asked.

"Eddie Jarvis. And yes, he's the same

one Harry picked out. We'll start tracking known associates and see what comes up."

"He's not a local," Harry said. "If he were a local, I'd know him."

Ramona didn't want to think about the kinds of people Harry might come across on a daily basis during the course of his work.

"You're right," the sergeant said, packing up his laptop. "He's got a very long rap sheet and multiple agencies are looking for him. He goes where the money is. And he'll hire out to do absolutely anything if the price is right."

"Are you saying he's the bigger danger now, not Darrin?" Ramona asked.

"No." The sergeant stopped and turned just before he reached the front door. "I'm saying that while Darrin is apparently motivated by hatred toward you, this guy is motivated by money. And it appears that Darrin has a lot of money. He could be hiring even more people to come after you. Be careful."

Bergman left and Ramona turned to Harry. "Now that we've helped identify this guy, maybe that will help speed things up and this nightmare will be over."

"Right," Harry said. He was nodding slightly in agreement, but the worried expression on his face told a whole different story.

"Considering that the databases the police are able to access haven't turned up a property purchase by Linder, it makes sense that even as a realtor, you wouldn't be able to, either," Harry said into his phone.

On the other end of the call, Caleb Petrov let out a frustrated exhale. "Lots of people buy properties through corporations and other means to hide their identity. I just figured there was a chance that Darrin might have been in too much of a hurry to cover his tracks very well, or maybe he hadn't thought ahead and made a purchase on impulse."

Harry leaned back in the slightly squeaky office chair and sighed. "Well, I appreciate your making the effort."

He was in the office at North Star Ranch with Adam and Ramona. Jay had gone into town to pick up some pizzas for lunch just before Harry and Ramona returned from Jasmine's condo. A couple of empty pizza boxes lay open on desktops. Cassie and the other two bounty hunters were out tracking a bail jumper who'd been spotted at the truck stop on the Idaho-Washington state line. Sherry and Jay were eating at the table in the dining room, surrounded by paperwork and a couple of electronic tablets as they worked on the monthly bills to be sent out to the people who boarded their animals at the ranch.

Adam's dogs were also in the office, lying near their master's feet, chewing on the treats Adam had just given them.

Tinker, the younger and smaller dog, was especially excited and kept rolling on his back and kicking his back legs while he chewed. His hind paws smacked Duke in the face several times. More than ten times Tinker's weight, Duke barely seemed to notice. He closed his eyes as if in exasperation when the little dog went into a kicking frenzy, but he didn't get up and move away.

"I really want to help get Darrin locked up," Caleb said over the phone. "My brother made some stupid decisions. He should never have tried drugs and he knows that now—but he wouldn't have done it if he hadn't been pressured into it. It just makes me so angry to know that Darrin and people like him make money exploiting other people's vulnerabilities. And they bring added violence to an otherwise nice town and put innocent people in danger." He sighed. "I'm emailing you a link that might help you."

Harry watched his computer screen

until he saw the notification and opened the email. "Got it," he said. It was a list of addresses and hyperlinks.

"I researched property listings going back to the time frame when Darrin first contacted me," Caleb said. "I looked for the elements he wanted. Then I looked to see which listings are no longer on the market. That's the list I just sent you. I can't find Darrin's name connected to any of the properties, but like we were just discussing, he could easily hide his connection. It's possible he actually did buy one of them."

"I could go out to the properties and have a look," Harry said. He was already clicking on the links and looking at the photos of lakeside houses with private piers and large storage buildings.

"I thought you might want to do that," Caleb said. "I've got to get back to work. Call me if there's anything else you need from me." He disconnected.

Harry set his phone down on the desk

and then leaned back with his arms crossed. His gaze was directed toward his computer screen but his thoughts were on the secluded locations of the properties on the list and he asked himself if this was yet another trap. He would not make the same mistake he'd made in Bridger. And that meant he couldn't blindly accept Caleb's help without questioning it.

What did he know about Caleb, really? How did Harry know if any of the man's story was true? For all Harry knew, this guy could be a plant sent by Darrin. He could even be a drug addict himself, wanting to keep Darrin from being caught so his supply of drugs wouldn't be interrupted.

There were so many angles to consider in this case. Harry couldn't afford to rush and make mistakes. And yet, he didn't have the luxury of leisurely mulling things over, either. He had to make decisions and he had to take action. Every minute that Darrin Linder walked free meant he could try again to kill Ramona. And Harry couldn't let that happen.

"What was that call about?" Ramona asked. "It sounded like you were talking to Caleb." She'd been sitting at Cassie's desk but got up and came to stand behind Harry, looking over his shoulder at the images he was clicking through.

Harry filled her in on Caleb's side of the conversation.

"We still have a few hours of daylight," Ramona said, glancing toward a window. "We could go check out one or two of the addresses."

"You two can't go alone," Adam said, getting to his feet and picking up the empty pizza boxes. "You need somebody watching your backs."

"Exactly what I was thinking," Harry said. "Much as I'd like to get this wrapped up right now, we'd better wait until Cassie and the guys are available and can go with us."

Adam nodded. "That would be my suggestion." He headed out of the room. The dogs picked up their toys and followed him.

"Just to be on the safe side, we won't look at the properties in the same order that they're listed here," Harry said, strategizing out loud. "We'll check them out in a random pattern. That way it won't be easy for someone to predict where we'll be next and set up an ambush."

"I think we should forward the information to Sergeant Bergman," Ramona said.

"Agreed." Harry forwarded the info along with a short explanation. "It's not exactly a hot tip," he said to Ramona. "I wouldn't expect Bergman to jump right on it. We'll probably end up checking it out before the police department does."

Ramona sat back down at Cassie's desk. She gestured toward a framed picture of Cassie with a uniformed cop. "I assume that's Cassie and her late husband. Do you know what happened to him?"

Harry stood up and walked over behind Ramona and looked at the picture. He'd seen it countless times, but it still tugged at his heart. Cassie and her husband, standing in the front room of this ranch house, both laughing.

"He was an Idaho state trooper," Harry said. "Whether that was related to his murder, no one knows. He had a Saturday off and he went fishing in one of the inlets on Lake Bell. He headed out early in the morning. Late that afternoon some hikers found him. He'd been shot. He'd apparently passed away several hours before they found him."

Ramona turned to him with emotion-filled eyes. "I remember back when that happened, it was all over the news. But I didn't make the connection until now. Did the police capture whoever killed him?"

"No." Harry shook his head. "There never were any useful leads. It's been four years since it happened and unfortunately, the case is stone-cold."

Harry had known about the murder of Cassie's husband. Nearly everybody in town did. But it had happened before they'd begun working together—back when they were nothing more than nodding acquaintances who recognized each other from their search-and-rescue volunteering.

Even though they were good friends now, he and Cassie still didn't talk much about their personal losses. They just didn't have that kind of relationship. But Cassie had pushed him when he needed it. Encouraged him to keep himself busy and she'd offered him meaningful work when he was floundering after losing Willa. He could only imagine her own experience with loss had taught her when to offer a helping hand.

"I don't know how Cassie was able to keep going after experiencing something like that," Ramona said. "I don't know how you were able to recover after losing your wife."

"You get through it the same way we're going to capture Darrin Linder and lock him up," Harry said. "One step at a time."

She smiled gently at him and gave him an encouraging nod.

And, if you're smart, he thought, *you protect your heart so you don't ever have to go through that kind of terrible loss ever again.*

ELEVEN

The next day, Harry, Ramona, Leon and Martin set out to take a look at the properties Caleb had listed.

By the time they drove up to the sixth property, Ramona had gotten used to the routine Harry had set up. They'd traveled back and forth around the perimeter of Lake Bell and it was already late into the afternoon. As Harry promised last night, he'd made a point of visiting the properties in a random order. And they had not visited properties that were close together one after another. He seemed determined to avoid making their movements predictable.

Ramona was sitting beside Harry in his truck, trying to resist that sense of connection with him and the almost physical tugging sensation that made her want to believe they belonged together.

Leon and Martin were in the big SUV. Cassie was working at the office in town.

Harry had made it clear when they first started out that not only did they want to stay hidden from Darrin and his thugs, but they wanted to stay out of sight of any neighbors or passersby, as well. If they were seen, there was the risk of the person telling Darrin that they'd seen someone prowling around his property.

They didn't have the time to park far away and hike to the fairly remote properties they were checking on in *full stealth mode* as Martin had called it. Instead, they stationed their vehicles at a point closest to the properties where they could pull off the road and keep the truck and SUV camouflaged by the surrounding thick forest of trees.

Lake Bell was ringed by steep hills rising just a few miles away, and the late afternoon sunlight was casting deep shadows through the low-lying section of forest where they were parked not far from the water's edge. They weren't especially close to the cabin campgrounds where Darrin and his goons had chased Ramona only eight days ago, but the scenery was so similar that she found herself thinking about that terrifying night. A shiver passed through her and she hugged herself. She'd spent so much time around the lake as a kid and thought of it as a fun, happy place to be. But now, thanks to Darrin Linder, being here left her feeling edgy and nervous.

"If you want me to take you back to the ranch, I will," Harry said, watching her closely.

It was amazing how often he seemed to know what she was feeling or what was on her mind. And looking into his honest blue eyes filled with concern, her skin warmed and her heart felt like it was starting to soften.

No. She commanded herself to stop. *He isn't ready to move on. He doesn't want to risk loving again. And you can't do anything to change that.*

Denying that truth and trying to press on toward a relationship with him would only make them both miserable. And yet, sitting here so close to him, breathing in the slight sandalwood scent of his aftershave, looking at the expression of genuine concern on his rugged face, made it hard to resist trying.

"After this one, we've only got one more property to check on, right?" she said, putting a lot of effort into sounding normal when she was feeling anything but. "I can make it." And after that, she should probably avoid being in close quarters with him. Her heart could only take so much.

She glanced out the window, watching Leon and Martin exit their vehicle, cross the road and disappear into the woods beside the house. Leon would be looking for fresh tire tracks or footprints near the entrances to the house and the big storage building. Martin would check out the private pier and boat house looking for watercraft, fuel containers or anything else that made it look like boats might be actively moving in and out of the dock.

Two of the properties they'd already checked on were occupied by what looked like typical families. In each case, Leon had taken pictures and short videos of the people he'd seen and texted them to Ramona for a quick look. She was the person who'd had the clearest views of Skinny Guy, whose real name still hadn't been determined, and Eddie Jarvis, formerly known as Bald Guy. Ramona was the one most likely to recognize them. And maybe, if Darrin had other partners with him, they might look familiar to her. There was the possibility that they would be people she'd seen with him before, while he was still dating Jasmine.

"I've got something." Leon's deep voice came across Harry's radio.

Ramona felt nerves tingle along the length of her spine. She wanted Darrin captured. But the thought that he might be nearby frightened her to her core. She didn't want to see his face. And absolutely didn't want to look into his eyes.

"What have you got?" Harry asked.

"The grass is packed down alongside the driveway near the front of the house," Leon reported. "And there are tire ruts in the dirt, too. It looks like there were several vehicles parked out here not long ago. I'm going to look a little more."

"Okay."

"What if somebody is living here now and Leon startles them?" Ramona asked. "He *is* trespassing. Somebody might come out shooting."

"We always run the risk that someone will shoot first and ask questions later," Harry said. "Most of the time we're hunting for dangerous people, so we're used to that. And as far as trespassing goes, you're right. But we aren't looking in windows. And if anyone other than Darrin or one of his thugs asks Leon to leave, he absolutely will. Immediately. And he'll offer an apology. We're assertive because we have to be. But it's never our intention to frighten or be rude to an innocent party."

Ramona nodded, thinking about how the world around her was not nearly as safe or fair or controllable as she would like it to be. She'd been reminded of that a lot lately.

"Martin, are you seeing this?" Leon's voice came over the radio.

"The boat?" Martin asked, speaking into his radio barely above a whisper. "Yeah. I'm trying to see if there's someone inside."

"What's going on?" Harry asked.

"I walked around the storage building

and saw a boat tied at the pier," Leon said. "If I move in a little closer, I might have a better view inside the wheelhouse than Martin."

"Stay cool," Harry said into the radio. "And be careful." He turned to Ramona. "We need to head over to the property. Just in case there's trouble."

He opened his door and got out. She swallowed nervously and followed suit. Part of her wanted to turn around and flee, but she reminded herself that Harry had given her every opportunity to remain back at the ranch. She'd come along because she honestly thought she could help them identify the bad guys. The potential for danger on this excursion had been made abundantly clear to her. Never more so than when she'd been handed bulletproof body armor.

Harry checked his sidearm and his taser, and then hung a set of binoculars around his neck. Ramona took a deep breath and silently prayed, *Dear Lord, please protect all of us.*

"Do you have your phone with you?" Harry asked as they started walking toward the property.

Ramona patted the thigh pocket on the khaki cargo pants Cassie had loaned her. "Yep, it's right here."

"Good. Now, stay behind me."

"Okay," she said.

They crossed the road and headed toward the side of the house closest to the storage building, paralleling the driveway as they threaded their way through the thick trees. Ramona saw the roof of the storage building first, off to her right. Then, to her left, she saw a low, rambling ranch-style house. Between them, she could see an expanse of the lake.

She heard five rapid gunshots from the side of the house that faced the lake.

And then an engine started up.

"Martin. Leon. Check in," Harry commanded into his radio. He reached behind him for Ramona's hand, grabbed it, and started running toward the house. They crouched down alongside a wall for cover.

It seemed to Ramona like it took forever for anyone to respond to Harry's call.

"They spotted us." Martin's voice finally came through the radio. "At least two men. They're in the boat. I'm with Leon. As soon as we started to move toward the boat, they started shooting. They've got us pinned down."

"Is Darrin Linder one of the men?" Harry asked.

"We can't tell," Martin answered.

Harry crept closer to the corner of the house and Ramona stayed right behind him, peering over his shoulder until they finally reached a point where she could see the boat, about a hundred feet away. In the fading light, she could just make out someone crouching down low on the bow and casting off the tie lines. The boat started to move away from its mooring.

"Hold your positions," Harry said. "And keep your heads down."

He lifted the binoculars off of his neck and handed them to Ramona. "See if you recognize anyone on the boat."

She wasn't used to using binoculars and the boat was bobbing up and down as it moved away from the pier. The fading sunlight wasn't helping, either, but finally her eyes landed on a sickeningly familiar face with unforgettable tattoos inked onto a thick neck. "Eddie Jarvis," she said. He was piloting the boat.

And then she saw the gun pointed in her direction. Heart thundering in her chest, she managed to grab Harry's arm and yank him out of the way before bullets tore off the corner of the house. Shaking at the near miss, Ramona found herself unable to loosen her grip on Harry.

"Leon, call 9-1-1," Harry said into the radio. "Report shots fired, and positive identification of a suspect wanted for the violent attacks on Ramona."

"I saw Skinny Guy, too," Ramona said. Her throat was so constricted by fear that she found it hard to force the words out. "That's who shot at us."

"Make that *two* suspects," Harry said into the radio.

"Got it," Leon said.

"Is one of the suspects Darrin Linder?" Martin asked.

"No," Harry said into the radio.

"I'm on the phone with 9-1-1," Leon said. "PD is coming by land. The sheriff's department is dispatching their patrol boat."

"Good. Now come meet up with us." Harry described their location, and a couple of minutes later Leon and Martin walked up to them.

Meanwhile, the boat had cleared the pier and was heading out toward the open lake at full throttle. With the sun just about to disappear behind the western peaks of the surrounding hills, much of the shoreline was already hidden in darkness. Lake Bell was big. Depending on where the sheriff's patrol boat was when they received the dispatch, it could take them a while to get here. The bad guys could be long gone.

"They're getting away," Ramona said sadly.

Harry wrapped an arm around her shoulder. "They'll only get away if we stop looking. And we *won't* stop looking for them. That's a promise."

"Well, we got some guns off the streets thanks to the efforts of you and your team," Sergeant Bergman said to Harry. "That'll likely save lives. I know what you really wanted was to capture Darrin Linder and his associates, but you still accomplished something substantial."

Maybe so, Harry thought. *But I'm not sure it made Ramona any safer.*

They were still at the lakeside property. It was after sunset and the surrounding forest was dark, but the exterior lights of the house and the outbuildings were on. The police were checking the storage building where they had found the guns, as well as looking through the garage and the boat shed for any additional evidence. Bergman was waiting to hear back from his commanding officer on whether he could breach the door and go into the house legally.

Cassie had arrived and she and Ramona were walking aimlessly around the stretch of lawn illuminated by the lights attached to the eaves of the house. Ramona had been shaky in the aftermath of the shooting and Cassie was calming her down.

Harry had wanted to do that, to offer Ramona comfort and reassurance, but that had seemed like a bad idea. He'd made himself a promise that he would put some emotional distance between them and he needed to stick to that. Although when bullets were flying, keeping his distance had been the last thing on his mind.

"Have you heard anything back from the deputies on the patrol boat?" Leon asked Bergman as he and Martin walked up. The two bounty hunters had been helping the police officers load the recovered firearms into a police department van. Then they'd joined the cops in doing a sweep of the grounds for any evidence that might have been left behind,

"Unfortunately, the pursuit across the lake was pretty much over before it even started." Bergman's normally unemotional tone had a bitter cast to it. "The sheriff's department only had the one boat on the lake today, and it was docked too far away when they got the call. By the time they made it over here, it was too dark to see anything."

"Can't you get a helicopter or a drone to look for them?" Martin asked.

Harry noticed the smallest hint of a smile at the corner of the sergeant's lips before the cop said, "The Stone River PD doesn't have a drone." His expression immediately went back to being all business. "But we will have the sheriff's department helicopter out here at first light tomorrow morning looking for them. If they approach someone's private dock tonight, odds are pretty good that the property owner will call us. If they try to moor in an isolated area, they still need to get to shore, get to a road and then have someone pick them up. With the weather still chilly and the water in the lake very cold, they'd be fools to jump overboard and try to swim to land and escape that way. They'd end up with hypothermia in no time."

"Is anybody claiming they *aren't* fools?" Ramona asked. She'd walked up with Cassie and heard the last of the sergeant's comments.

"I get what you mean," Harry said. "They're criminals and they've obviously made extremely bad life choices. But they aren't stupid. If Darrin had hired some local small-time thugs to work with him, we would have caught them by now. But he hired pros."

"Eddie Jarvis is a career criminal for certain," Bergman said. "I imagine the skinny guy is, too. But that will just make it all the sweeter when we catch them. And when we have them, we'll use them to get Darrin."

Bergman's phone rang. He excused himself and stepped away to take the call.

Harry looked around at Cassie, Ramona, Leon and Martin and let out a sigh.

"Everybody's safe and sound," Cassie said, catching Harry's eye and directing the words to him, like a reminder. He was indeed relieved that Ramona and his crew were in good shape and unharmed. But Darrin and his henchmen were still at large, which meant Harry couldn't relax. The fact that Darrin had hired good help showed that he really was trying to build a criminal empire. And that he wasn't going to give up and go away.

Over by the front door of the house, Bergman called out to his officers that they'd gotten a warrant and it was time to go inside and conduct a search.

"I hope they find something that helps with the case," Martin said.

Leon nodded. "Maybe they will."

"Dad's keeping dinner warm for us back at the ranch," Cassie said, glancing at a text on her phone. "There's nothing else for us to do here. We might as well head home."

They walked back to their vehicles.

"You're pretty quiet," Harry said to Ramona after the two of them were buckled up in his truck. "Are you all right?" He started the engine, and then pulled out onto the road behind Cassie but in front of Martin and Leon, so that he and Ramona were in the protected center of their short caravan.

"They could be anywhere," Ramona finally said.

Harry glanced over and saw her looking out her side window, toward the darkness.

"Darrin. His two thugs. Anyone else he might have hired. They can go wherever they want to go, do whatever they want to do. Commit crimes. Hurt people. It isn't fair." She shook her head.

"No, it's not," Harry agreed. He understood her frustration. Most people didn't have to deal with crime all that much. But when you did have to deal with it on a regular basis, it could get to you. And he knew that was what was happening to Ramona.

She was knotting her hands in her lap, and he very nearly reached over to rest his hand on top of hers. But he caught himself at the last second. "I know things can look hopeless. And unfortunately, it's true that we don't win every battle."

"If you're trying to cheer me up, you aren't doing a very good job."

"The bright side is that while there are people determined to do evil things, there are also people determined to do good. And sometimes we prevail."

He glanced over at her and she was looking at him. "Still not cheered up," she said.

He could understand that. And while he wanted to make her feel better, he also didn't want to lie to her. He really had no idea how this case was going to play out or what was going to happen next. But he was pretty certain that now that they had found Darrin's *lair* and taken away the guns he'd obviously intended to sell, he would be looking for payback. And things might get rough. Well, rough*er*.

"You already know that Adam's an excellent cook. Does the thought of a good dinner cheer you up?"

This time she laughed softly. "Okay, that does help a little."

Harry smiled and tried to make himself look relaxed. Meanwhile, he kept a wary eye on approaching traffic as they continued down the road. Just in case. Because

Ramona was right. The bad guys could be anywhere. And going forward, they truly needed to be ready for anything.

TWELVE

Harry opened the door of the Rock Solid
Bail Bonds office to let Sergeant Bergman step inside. The cop typically kept
his facial expression neutral, but on this
visit, Harry saw concern in his eyes.
After the officer stepped over the thresh-
old, Harry closed the door behind him,
flipped over the sign beside the door so
it read CLOSED and then dropped the
blinds so that they covered the windows
facing Centennial Street.

"Have you found the guys who took off
on the boat?" Ramona asked. She had a
strained but slightly hopeful expression
on her face as she walked up to the sergeant.

The twenty-four hours since the showdown at the lakeside house had been tense. Everyone at North Star Ranch knew to be on their guard, even though there were no signs that Darrin or his accomplices knew Ramona was staying there. It simply wasn't worth taking the chance.

"Who else is here?" Bergman asked before answering Ramona's question.

Harry glanced past Ramona at Cassie, Leon and Martin. "Just the five of us."

They'd come downtown to the office earlier in the day because business outside of this case had to continue. Though the recent events with Darrin and his henchmen over the last week were far from normal, danger came with the territory. Everyone on staff knew how to set aside their anxieties and focus on the job at hand when they had to.

Cassie needed to keep the doors open if she wanted to write new bonds and stay in business. Plus, she'd had a couple of high-flight-risk clients with upcoming court dates that she wanted to keep track of by having them physically check in.

Harry and Leon had both asked informants they used on occasion to stop by so they could find out if anybody had seen Linder or his accomplices since last night. They'd learned that word was out all over town about Darrin expanding his drug business and moving into weapons dealing, but the informants hadn't seen Darrin himself and didn't know anyone who had.

Cassie and the bounty hunters had been discussing further options for tracking him down when Sergeant Bergman had called Ramona. After learning she was at the bail bonds office, he'd told her he wanted to come over to talk with her and the bounty hunters.

When Bergman sat down on the sofa, he set down an electronic tablet on the coffee table. Ramona sat down to his left. Harry sat down on his right. The others remained standing, taking up positions behind the couch so that they'd be able to see the tablet screen.

"What's up?" Ramona asked, nervously rubbing her hands together.

"We believe we have found the two men from the boat last night," Bergman said. "I'm assuming they're the same two perps who've had a hand in attacking you from the very beginning. I'm going to need you to positively identify them."

"Were you able to get them to talk?" Ramona asked quickly. "Did they tell you where Darrin is? Are they willing to testify against him?"

"That's not going to be possible," Bergman said heavily.

Harry had a feeling he knew what was coming.

"They're dead," Bergman said.

Yeah, that was what Harry figured Bergman was going to say. Harry shifted his gaze toward Ramona and his gut twisted as he saw the color drain from her face.

"What happened?" she whispered, obviously shocked.

"We found them on the south side of the lake. They were both killed execution style. A guy who lives out that way was jogging with his dogs this morning. The dogs started acting strange, howling and pulling on their leashes, so he followed them into the trees. He saw two bodies lying there and called us."

"But...what? Why?" Ramona sputtered as if too many thoughts were colliding in her mind for her to give clear voice to any of them.

Harry glanced over his shoulder and made eye contact with Cassie and Leon. Both gave him a slight nod, which meant they were as worried as he was. Martin had his gaze on Bergman.

"Any idea what happened?" Harry asked the sergeant.

"The boat the two men escaped in was moored at a private pier. We've checked out the owner of the property and we're convinced he had no connection to Linder or his criminal enterprise. Footprints leading up to the road from the pier, plus fresh tire tracks alongside the road, suggest that they called Linder to get them and when he arrived, he shot and killed them."

"How can you be certain it was Darrin who did it?" Cassie asked.

"I'll get to that." Bergman reached for the tablet on the table and tapped the screen to wake it. "I have some things to show you," he said to Ramona.

Ramona was the one who'd been targeted from the beginning. Harry and the rest of the team had jumped in to help keep her safe and capture the bad guys, but at the end of the day, she was at the center of it all. She was the one who absolutely deserved to be kept informed. She was the one who needed to know that the police were taking her case seriously and doing their best to get justice for her.

The sergeant never lost sight of that and Harry respected him all the more for it.

"I have pictures of the two men, and I need you to confirm that they were the ones who were involved in the shooting last night as well as the earlier attacks. It's a required procedure. I'd like your confirmation because you had the binoculars and had the clearest view of them last night."

"Are they pictures from the scene when their bodies were found?" Ramona asked hesitantly.

"They are not. They're booking photos taken when the men were arrested for previous crimes. We were able to pull prints to identify them positively."

First came the photo of Eddie Jarvis without his snake tattoos. Ramona quickly confirmed he was the thug she'd seen through the binoculars last night and that he'd been in the boat's wheelhouse. Next came the photo of Skinny Guy. The man who'd used the alias of Albert

Mason when he'd rented the cabin at the Western Trails Resort. His real name was Jaron Carroll. Ramona confirmed that she'd also seen him through the binoculars and that he was the man who'd shot at her and Harry from the boat, as well as being involved in the earlier attacks.

"Now that we have that done, I'll get back to Cassie's question about how we know Darrin was responsible for the executions." He glanced over his shoulder at Cassie and others. "You're going to want to see this."

Then he turned around, tapped the screen a couple of times, and a video started. "This is from the security system on the property where the stolen boat was moored," he said.

The video gave a relatively wide-angle view and started with the boat tied at the pier. The two thugs got out of the boat, walked the length of the pier and then started walking up the slight hill toward the road. They were moving quickly and looking around furtively as one of them talked on his cell phone. Soon, they were out of view.

Bergman fast-forwarded the video until it reached a point where Darrin Linder came into view. He was walking down the slight hill and toward the boat. He was alone, with a pistol in his hand.

"I'm assuming you've enlarged that image, identified the type of gun and matched the caliber of ammo to the gunshot evidence you found at the scene," Leon said.

Bergman nodded. "Of course."

A few seconds later in the video, Darrin climbed out of the boat carrying two large backpacks.

"We suspect the backpacks contain illegal drugs," Bergman said. "Or possibly cash. Or guns. Maybe all three. It looks like the two accomplices were so anxious to get away from the boat and make their escape that they left them behind. So, Linder went back for them."

As Darrin walked by the camera again, he appeared to notice it for the first time. He stopped, peered at it and then moved closer. At that point, he offered up a chilling smile.

His cheeks were sunken and the expression in his eyes made him appear feverish.

"What's he doing?" Ramona asked.

"That is the face of a man who has snapped," Cassie said.

Bergman nodded.

In the video, Darrin held up the pistol and blew at the barrel as if he were blowing away smoke. And then he said something, but the video didn't include sound.

"What's he saying?" Martin asked.

"And why would he kill his own men?" Ramona added.

"We think he's saying, 'I love you, Jasmine,'" Bergman said. He did a quick rewind, and from what Harry could see, it looked like those words matched the movement of Linder's lips.

"Have you told Jasmine about this?" Ramona asked.

"Yes. We warned her that Linder is an ongoing threat to her safety, and that he's definitely still in the area. She says her recently installed security system is working well and that she doesn't leave her home without a friend or coworker by her side."

The video played out with Darrin waving goodbye with his gun in his hand before turning and walking out of the frame of the camera.

Bergman turned to Ramona. "Darrin Linder appears to be a drug dealer who uses his own product, and that never ends well. Cassie's right, he's fallen off the edge. He's taunting the authorities in this tape because he believes he's invincible, which is a common side effect of a lot of illicit drugs. And I think he believes his actions here will impress your cousin and help him win her back."

Ramona hugged herself. Harry thought it was for the best that he wasn't sitting next to her. If he were, he wouldn't have been able to resist the temptation to wrap his arm around her shoulder, hold her close and do everything he could to make her feel safe. But that would send mixed signals about his intentions once this case was wrapped up. He did not plan to pursue any kind of relationship with her—not even friendship, even though he wanted it. She deserved more than he could give her. She deserved to have a man in her life who could offer her a future. And he was not that man.

"As far as a motive for Linder to murder his cohorts, the fact that he's under the influence of drugs and appears to be having some sort of mental breakdown could be motive enough," Bergman said to Ramona. "Or he could have done it on impulse, with no motive at all, for the exact same reason. Maybe he was mad at Eddie and Jaron because they left those bags behind on the boat. Or he could have decided that the shoot-out last night somehow made them too great a liability. He could have been angry that they hadn't killed or kidnapped you yet and decided that he was finished with them."

Fear, cold and sharp, settled in the center of Harry's chest. "That video demonstrates that Darrin is still fixated on Jasmine," he said. "We have to assume that he's also still fixated on Ramona as the biggest obstacle to winning Jasmine back." The thought of what that lunatic might do to Ramona had the hairs on the back of Harry's neck standing on end.

"That's precisely why I wanted you all to see the video for yourself instead of just telling you about it." The sergeant got to his feet and picked up the tablet. "I don't want to imply that you haven't been vigilant in protecting Ramona..." He swept his glance across the room, directing his comments to everyone. "But now more than ever, you need to stay mindful of just how dangerous this situation is."

* * *

"I can't stop shaking." Valerie Castillo sat perched on the edge of an old folding chair in the office of Kitchen Table.

"Let me help you with that." Worried that her aunt's shaking hands would result in her accidently burning herself, Ramona reached for the freshly filled coffee cup in Valerie's hand, poured a little of it into an empty mug sitting on a desk and then handed the cup back to her.

Ramona had been at the bounty hunter office, still thinking about the video Sergeant Bergman had shown them an hour earlier, when her dad called. Aunt Valerie had shown up at the diner in a panic, he told her, saying Darrin Linder had threatened to kill her. While still on the phone, Ramona had turned to Harry and told him what was happening.

"Have them call the cops," he said. Then he grabbed both his coat and hers from the coatrack and headed toward the door. "Let's go."

They arrived fifteen minutes later, and Valerie was still having trouble focusing her thoughts. Toni had suggested the cup of coffee. Now that Valerie was taking her second and third sips, she seemed to be calming a little.

"You're sure you're all right?" Toni stood by, anxiously twisting one of the diner's blue-and-white striped dish towels in her hands. "Darrin didn't hurt you?"

Valerie nodded. "I'm okay. He didn't touch me." She reached for the coffee, used both hands to try to hold it steady and took a noisy slurp. Eric stepped into the office and turned to his sister-in-law. "Sergeant Bergman will be here in a few minutes. I told him Jasmine should be home from work by now and he said he'd have a patrol car dispatched to park outside her condo and keep an eye on things."

"I haven't even told Jasmine about this yet." Valerie's voice was still a little shaky. "She's trying so hard, maintaining her job while doing her outpatient rehab work. I don't want her to have a setback."

"So, what exactly happened?" Ramona asked, rolling over an office chair and sitting in it so she was face-to-face with her aunt. Normally Valerie looked so confident, so put-together. It was unusual to see her looking this uncertain and vulnerable. It was also a reminder that everyone was vulnerable to cracking under sufficient pressure. It wasn't just Jasmine who had to struggle to hold herself together sometimes.

"I came home from work," Valerie said, clutching the now-empty coffee cup tightly. "I unlocked the front door, walked inside and set my purse and keys on the table in the entryway like I always do. It wasn't dark yet, but it was getting dusky. So, I walked into the front room and flicked on the lights. And then I saw him."

"Darrin?" Toni asked. "Right there in your front room?"

"Not exactly. When I looked across the front room, I could see him sitting at my dining room table. He had a gun pointed at me."

"What did he say?" Harry asked.

"It was so strange," Valerie said, shaking her head as if baffled by the memory. "He was smiling. Like he was happy to see me. He gestured for me to come closer. He had the gun pointed at me and I was afraid he was going to shoot me, so I did what he asked. Then he had me sit down at the table with him. He said, 'I love Jasmine and we're going to be married.' And then he told me if I didn't convince Jasmine to meet with him within twenty-four hours, he'd kill me."

She choked back a sob, took a couple of breaths to calm herself and then continued. "It was weird... His tone was so reasonable and polite the whole time. He said that he and Jasmine had had some troubles, but all of that was behind them now." Valerie turned to Ramona. "He said that you tried to break them up, but that you'd be out of the way very soon."

Ramona's hands began to tremble. She looked to Harry, who was standing nearby, but he didn't offer a comforting touch or give her the look that gave her a feeling of connection with him. Her heart sank, even though she knew she needed to concentrate on her aunt and not on herself. His withdrawal felt like one more measure of sadness added to an already horrible day.

Toni covered her mouth with her hand and then turned to look at Ramona with tear-filled eyes. Eric walked over and put his arm around his wife's shoulder.

"Sorry," Valerie said, looking down. "Maybe I shouldn't have mentioned that part."

"Don't be sorry," Ramona said. "You didn't do anything wrong. It's better to hear everything, so we know what we're dealing with. Please, keep going with your story."

"There's not much more to tell. He took the house phone I keep in the kitchen and broke it. He made me get my phone out of my purse and he broke that, too. Then he made me get in the hall closet and he pushed some furniture up against the door. At first, I was too afraid to do anything. And then, after some time passed, I knew he must have left. So, I started trying to get the door open. I pushed against it, and bit by bit the furniture moved out of the way. Eventually I got the door open and I got out." Tears began to roll down her cheeks. "I was so scared. I just grabbed my car keys and came straight over here."

Toni walked over and wrapped her arms around her sister. "I'm so glad you did."

A few minutes later Sergeant Bergman walked into the small office.

Ramona stood up and offered the sergeant her chair so he could interview Valerie. The diner's office was feeling too crowded; her heart was beating too quickly, and a thrashing feeling began to rise up in her chest. She was on the edge of panic. She could feel it taking over her body like a fever. The terror and the dread and the anxiety of the last week was all too much.

She hurried out to the kitchen. Feeling Harry walking behind her, she spoke over her shoulder, "I need some fresh air." She reached to open the back door.

"Hold on a minute." Harry moved in front of her, opened the door about an inch and turned around so he was standing in front of it. "There's your fresh air," he said. "If you were planning to step outside for a few minutes, I don't think that's a good idea."

She could feel cooler evening air drifting into the warm kitchen, and it did help. The panicky feeling began to subside. She looked up at Harry, and despite everything going on between them, or maybe everything *no longer* going on between them, he was still steady and solid and looking out for her.

"How do you do it?" she asked, her voice sounding tight and croaky with anxiety. "How do you hold it together?"

"I don't know that I always do," Harry said with a slight, self-conscious smile. "I think it's more that I've had enough life experience to realize how little I can control. And how much I need to lean on the Lord. That doesn't mean I don't try my hardest to take care of things. But I have the strength to keep trying because I know there's a higher plan even if I don't understand it. And I know all things work together for good in the end."

"I appreciate that sentiment," Ramona said. "I truly do. But I'd really like for things to work together for good *right now*."

And absurd as it might seem given the circumstances, she wanted things to work out between her and Harry. She already missed the small flirtations. Missed the lingering looks and the glancing touches that lasted a little longer than they really needed to.

From what he'd shared over the past several days, Ramona believed he had gotten closer to venturing back into the romantic world with her than he had with any other woman since his wife passed away. But apparently, he'd firmly decided that he didn't want to go any further. Maybe he didn't want to take the risk of loving someone and losing them like he had Willa. Or perhaps it was something about Ramona, personally, that didn't work for him.

What made it much more painful was that he was being such a gentleman about it. It would be easier to think about going their separate ways if he were a jerk. But he was still kind, still compassionate. Still protective. He would make a wonderful friend. But she couldn't go down that road with him. Telling herself she could be happy as nothing more than friends with Harry would be a lie. The truth was that she was in danger of falling in love with the man.

The *whole* truth was that she probably already had.

Painful as it would be to walk away from him after Darrin was captured—assuming she was still alive by then—she had to make a clean break. Otherwise, she could waste years hoping to change the man when it wasn't in her power to do that.

"Have you had enough fresh air?" Harry asked.

Ramona nodded and he closed the door and locked it.

From inside the office, Ramona heard Bergman say to Valerie, "I want you to know that capturing Darrin Linder is the number one priority for both the police department and the sheriff's department. We know Linder is dangerous and unpredictable. We've already contacted an FBI behavioral expert."

Ramona's parents stepped out of the office, looking pale and worried.

Ramona wanted to hope for the best, but right now that was really difficult. There had to be something she could do, some way she could help. She felt like she was caught in a trap, and that even if she were able to escape it, someone she loved was bound to get hurt. Maybe even killed.

THIRTEEN

"I'm glad you're doing okay," Ramona said to Jasmine, feeling a little bit dishonest even though she was telling the truth. She *was* happy—and relieved—that Jasmine was all right. But checking on her cousin's well-being wasn't really the reason for making the trip to the condo to see her.

Darrin's threats to Valerie last night had the whole family shaken up. Before everyone went their separate ways from the diner, there'd been discussion of how much to tell Jasmine. In the end, they decided that Jasmine deserved to know the whole truth. Ramona volunteered to call Jasmine and tell her what happened because Valerie was afraid she couldn't talk to her daughter without crying. She was afraid that hearing her cry would make Jasmine feel worse than she already did.

So Ramona explained it all and immediately reassured Jasmine that her mom was fine and staying with Ramona's parents at their house. Eric and Toni were going to stay home with her for a few days at Sergeant Bergman's recommendation—he thought all of them staying out of view was a good idea. He was positioning a patrol car outside of their house in case Darrin tried to make good on his threat on Valerie.

They wanted Jasmine to stay there, as well, but she tearfully refused. She'd said she was afraid she would draw danger to them.

When Jasmine finally broke up with Darrin, his behavior toward her quickly shifted. Toward the end of their relationship, he'd been abusive toward her, physically and verbally, but once she ended things, he'd eased up on the threats to her, redirecting them toward her family instead. Jasmine had been frightened and repelled, but because he'd kept his distance, she'd felt relatively safe at home and at work.

Until now. If Darrin was coming completely unhinged, it seemed likely he would give up all pretense of charming Jasmine into taking him back and instead just come after her. If he did, she didn't want her family to get hurt when that happened.

Jasmine had cried hard while Ramona was on the phone with her last night, and according to Valerie, she'd cried nearly the whole time she was on the phone with her mom. Ramona had wanted to stop by the condo and see her on the way back to the ranch with Harry last night, but he convinced her that it would be wiser if everyone went straight to where they were going for the night and stayed there.

Back at North Star Ranch, Adam had cooked yet another nice dinner. But stress and worry meant Ramona hadn't been able to eat more than a couple of bites. So, she'd moved the food around on her plate while she thought about what she could do to help capture Darrin.

A plan had started to take shape in her mind. It wasn't exactly something she *wanted* to do. In fact, she was afraid to do it. But it seemed like a good idea.

She knew she had a better chance of convincing Jasmine to work with her if she talked to her about it in person.

They moved to the kitchen. "I made a pot of coffee," Jasmine said, looking puffy-eyed. She glanced at Harry, who had arrived alongside Ramona. "I didn't get much sleep last night. I'm not going in to work today."

"I have an idea on how to bring all of this to an end," Ramona said, taking mugs out of the cabinet. At her direction, Harry took the cream out the fridge and then got the sugar dish out of the cabinet.

"What's your idea?" Jasmine asked.

"We're going to make Darrin think that he's finally getting a meeting with you. You'll call him to arrange it. But of course, you won't go. It'll be somebody else."

"Who?" Jasmine asked suspiciously. "You?"

In fact, that had been Ramona's original idea when she'd called Bergman last night to suggest her plan. She was terrified at the prospect; the last thing in the world she wanted to do was face Darrin Linder again. But her offer made sense. She looked a lot like Jasmine and could imitate her voice as well. She was the reasonable choice.

When Ramona had first mentioned the idea to Harry, he visibly blanched. And while he'd kept his usual calm, measured demeanor as he tried to talk her out of it, she'd been able to see the near-panic in his eyes.

In the end, though, it had been Bergman who'd been remarkably open-minded when she'd told him about her proposed plan. He had, however, insisted a police officer would be the bait. He wanted to meet with Jasmine first, make sure she was onboard with the plan and willing to help. And, he told Ramona bluntly, he wanted to make sure Jasmine wasn't still in love with Darrin. That she wouldn't be tempted to warn him away at the last minute.

"Sergeant Bergman wants to use an officer made up to look like you," Ramona said to Jasmine. "She might want to borrow one of your outfits to wear. Or maybe your jacket. Something Darrin would recognize." She glanced at the clock on the kitchen wall. "The sergeant should be coming here any minute now."

"What about me just doing it myself?" Jasmine said, her voice husky with regret. "I'm the one who started it all. I'm the one who should take the risk."

Ramona took in a deep breath and steeled her nerves. She'd been expecting this. She knew her cousin had a good heart and that she wouldn't want to put anyone else in danger. On the other hand, while Ramona didn't want to insult her, she honestly didn't think Jasmine was up to the task. She was too emotionally fragile. But how did she tell her without making her think Ramona didn't trust her?

Go with the truth. "Given everything you've been going through lately, I don't think that's a good idea. You don't want to take on too much and risk backsliding from the progress you've made."

Ramona held her breath and waited for Jasmine's reaction. Jasmine had held herself together remarkably well since turning her life around, and this morning she stayed true to form. Her eyes filled with tears that she impatiently wiped away and her shoulders sagged, but she nodded her understanding. "A cop would know way better than me how to handle the situation, anyway," she finally said.

"Good job," Harry whispered, so lightly

by Ramona's ear that it was barely more than an exhalation. She felt her heart twist in her chest. Despite her best efforts, she still felt like she and Harry were a team. More than a team. It was going to feel like she was losing a part of herself when the hunt for Darrin finished and they parted ways. His whisper of encouragement made that worse. And having him standing close enough that she smelled his aftershave didn't help any.

Ramona's phone chimed and she looked at the screen. "It's Bergman. He says he's approaching the front door."

Jasmine tapped the screen of her phone a couple of times, opening up the security system's app, and then showed Ramona and Harry the live video of the sergeant approaching the condo. The three of them grabbed their coffees, with Ramona pouring one more for Bergman, and they walked out to the front room.

"Your real estate informant, Caleb Petrov, has been reported missing by his wife," Bergman said as soon as he walked in the door. Ramona handed him a mug of coffee and he nodded in appreciation. "It's too soon to open a formal missing person's investigation. He's an adult and hasn't been missing for twenty-four hours yet. But his wife called the station an hour ago because she's very concerned. Caleb left for work this morning but he never showed up. He isn't answering his wife's calls. She knows Caleb was trying to help us find Linder. She's worried that Darrin somehow found out."

Ramona thought about kind, gentle Caleb being in danger and she felt her stomach drop. Beside her, Harry drew himself up, took a deep breath and squared his shoulders. She could tell by the expression on his face that he was ready to step in and do whatever he could to help.

Bergman turned to Jasmine. "I assume Ramona has told you about the plan to draw out Darrin Linder. Are you willing to help us?"

"I want to help," she answered with a firm nod.

"I need to know the truth. Do you still have feelings for Darrin?" Bergman asked. "Are you in communication with him? Are you going to try to warn him away from us?"

"You already know about the texts he's sent me. All from different numbers. I've reported to you every time he's made contact with me since all of this began because I want him locked up. And no, I have absolutely no intention of helping him."

"All right then," Bergman said. "Let's get this rolling. His threat to your mom had a timeline attached to it and I believe he'll follow through. I've already got some officers on standby, ready to go. Use the number from his most recent text. Call him instead of texting so he knows it's really you. Tell him you want to meet with him. Get him to set a location and a time. Put the phone on speaker."

She dialed the first number and it went to voice mail.

"Leave a message," Bergman whispered.

One by one, she called the other numbers from the text messages Darrin had sent over the last week, professing his love for her. No one answered any of them, so she left messages at each number.

With each call, the anxiety in the pit of Ramona's stomach ratcheted higher until it felt like her gut was in her throat.

Seconds after Jasmine left her last message, her phone chimed with a text message. "Cardinal and Sixth Street," she read aloud, her voice shaking. "Be there in fifteen minutes."

Ramona chilled. "That's way too soon, isn't it?" she said, looking at a grim-faced Bergman. "Your cops couldn't possibly be ready in time."

"Why do you think he's texting instead of talking?" Harry asked.

"He wants to keep the upper hand," Bergman said. "You can lose control of an actual conversation pretty quickly. With texts, he can keep a tighter rein on things and direct the conversation." He turned to Jasmine. "What's the significance of that location? Does it mean anything to you?"

"It's near Bear Hollow Deli, where we had our first lunch date."

"Call him back," Bergman said. "Tell him you need more time. Say that you're at work and you can't just run out the door."

Jasmine followed his instructions. Her phone chimed again. This time he sent her a picture. It was of Caleb, bruised, bleeding, tied up and shoved into the trunk of a car. It was followed by another text: Cardinal and Sixth. Be there in fifteen minutes or he dies.

"It's all my fault." Jasmine began crying and shaking.

Ramona drew in a deep breath. She had to step in. There was not enough time to do anything else. "Dear Lord, please help us," she whispered. Then she walked over to a kitchen drawer, pulled out a pair of scissors and handed them to Harry. "Cut my hair so I look more like Jasmine. Do it quickly. Then I'll leave to meet up with Darrin."

A hat wouldn't work. Jasmine didn't wear hats. And if Ramona was going to do this, she needed to be one hundred percent convincing.

Otherwise, she would be dead.

Harry sat in the unmarked cop car next to Bergman as they drove through downtown Stone River. The whole time, the sergeant stayed on his phone, coordinating a last-minute protective detail around the deli.

Harry stayed completely focused on

Ramona who was driving in front of them in Jasmine's car. She had Jasmine's phone with her in case Darrin sent any more texts. She also had her own phone, which was currently on a call with Harry's.

"You're doing great," Harry said into his phone. He had the call on speaker, and he forced himself to sound much calmer than he felt.

"Do you see Darrin?" she asked, her voice strained. "I don't see any sign of him."

They were nearing the intersection that Darrin had named, which meant they were close to the deli.

"Slow down," Bergman said to Ramona, having just finished his own call. "Darrin's probably set himself up nearby and he's likely watching you right now. Since he can see that 'Jasmine' is almost to the deli, it doesn't matter if you're a little late. So, take your time, and give my cops another minute to get in place."

Bergman had given Ramona a bulletproof vest to wear under Jasmine's purple jacket, but that didn't make Harry feel any better about her safety. He was sick with worry. It felt like he was going through the trauma of losing Willa all over again.

Stop. It's not the same thing. He needed to collect himself if he was going to be of any use to Ramona.

He wished he could take her place, that he could be the one in danger. He wished he could tell her how much he admired her. How much brighter his life had become since he'd met her, even with danger surrounding them the whole time. She was smart. She was funny. She was kind. It felt good to be near her, to breathe in her scent. He looked forward to seeing her every morning at the ranch. He loved having conversations and hearing her unique take on things.

He loved *her*.

Something like a cross between a

laugh and a moan escaped him. Bergman glanced over at him.

Harry shook his head. He was an idiot. He'd pushed Ramona away because he didn't want to get hurt. But it was way too late for that. Right now, she was in danger. If she got hurt, he wouldn't feel less anguish because he'd emotionally withdrawn from her. He'd feel intensely *more* anguish at the opportunity he'd wasted.

He'd decided he wasn't ready to heal from the loss of Willa and move forward with his romantic life again. But the joke was on him. It looked like that decision wasn't his to make.

Now he wanted nothing more than to wrap his arms around Ramona and tell her how much he loved her. Maybe she wouldn't care. He might have forever ruined his chance at a relationship with her when he'd taken that emotional step back. Fool that he was, he'd done it right when she needed him most. He wasn't sure she'd forgive him for that. He wasn't sure he'd forgive himself, either.

"Let me get out of the car when we get up here," Harry said to Bergman, gesturing toward the upcoming intersection. Harry had his sidearm, cuffs and pepper spray with him. He could get out of the car and run over to the deli. He'd find that little coward Darrin Linder and take him into custody before the scum had the chance to even lay eyes on Ramona. Harry had faced much more daunting adversaries in Afghanistan. He could take care of this situation.

"Sit tight," Bergman said to him in a steely voice.

Over the open line Harry had with Ramona, he heard her say, "Darrin's just sent another text. Now he wants Jasmine to head over to the lake, near where the dinner cruise boats dock."

"Start moving that way," Bergman said. "Slowly."

Harry turned to glare at him. It wasn't

the sergeant's fault that Darrin was playing games, but Harry was nevertheless furious with the situation.

Bergman was back on his phone with his officers telling them about the change in plans.

"Do you think Darrin's seen us and figured out that we're following her?" Harry asked.

"I don't know. But we're going to pull back and let another cop follow her for a bit just in case." Bergman slowed down. "This guy is one of ours." He let a silver pickup get in front of him, and then he made a turn that took him and Harry down a side street.

Having Ramona out of his sight made Harry feel like his heart had been ripped from his chest. He wanted to see everything as she arrived at the new location, so he could assess the situation and be ready to jump in and help however he was needed.

"Another text from Darrin," Ramona's

voice came over the speaker on Harry's phone. "It's another intersection. Ponderosa Road and Eighth Street."

"Do you have any idea what significance that location might have?" Harry asked her.

"No."

Bergman said to Ramona, "Start making your way in that direction." Once again, he updated his officers.

"Since the communications are by text, we don't even know for certain if they're really coming from Darrin," Harry said as Bergman steered through traffic.

"You're right," Bergman said. "And I've thought to myself more than once that there's got to be someone else involved with this. Or maybe several other people. His criminal enterprises have required him to buy drugs and weapons to resell, not to mention the house and the boat. That takes a lot of money. More than I'd expect him to have, no matter how well his drug dealing was going." The sergeant shook his head. "Maybe he's got ties to someone over in Seattle. That's where his hired help came from."

They reached the intersection from Darrin's text. Ramona had already parked on the street in front of an interior decorating shop. The silver truck that Bergman had assigned to keep tabs on her was a little farther down the street.

"I don't like this," Harry said to Ramona. Darrin's actions said that he was violent and delusional. He blamed Ramona for ruining his life. As long as he thought the woman arriving was Jasmine, she should be okay. But if Darrin realized she was actually Ramona, things could go very badly very quickly.

"I'm not crazy about this situation, either," Ramona replied. "But this is the first real chance we've had to capture Darrin since the night at the cabins. And Caleb Petrov's life is at stake. I have to do this."

Through the speaker, Harry could hear

a chime from Jasmine's phone. "Okay, a new text," Ramona said. "It says to go into the coffee shop, Mountain Peak Coffee. He says he's left a note there."

"Wait," Harry said, heart pounding. "Let's have one of the plainclothes cops go in first and look for him. Maybe they'll be able to arrest him and this will all be over."

"But he might not be inside the coffee shop," Ramona said. "He might be somewhere nearby, hiding and watching. Maybe he won't show himself until he sees 'Jasmine.' I can't let him get away. I'm going to go inside, take a quick look, and if I don't see him, I'll ask for the note."

"Look down and keep your face hidden as much as possible," Bergman said. "Don't give him a chance to see you aren't Jasmine."

Harry watched her get out of the car. She was vulnerable, possibly in Darrin's crosshairs right this very minute. He was shocked to realize he didn't regret losing his heart to her, even though that made him vulnerable to experiencing horrible loss all over again. What he regretted was not opening his heart sooner and telling her how he felt. If the worse thing imaginable came to pass, and Darrin Linder got to her before anyone could stop him, Harry's biggest regret would be that he never had the chance to tell her that he loved her.

FOURTEEN

Ramona slowly climbed out of the car. Her knees were shaking with adrenaline and fear. Once her feet were solidly on the pavement, she took a few seconds to just stand there and steady herself. Then she straightened the sunglasses she'd borrowed from Jasmine. One more trick, along with borrowing one of Jasmine's trendy outfits, to hide her identity.

She tried to draw in a deep, calming breath, but her lungs were tight and the air wouldn't come. She could only take shallow breaths. Whether that was from fear or from her asthma kicking in, she couldn't say. And now was not the time to let herself be distracted by digging

was going to happen here; she was sure of it. It made no sense for Darrin to leave a note with more directions. But then again, Darrin had stopped making sense a while ago.

Enough. She patted the phone in her pocket. The line was still open; hopefully Harry and Bergman could hear what was happening. Although with the buzz of conversation, the hissing from the espresso machines and the clanks and clatters from plates and mugs, she wondered if they could hear anything useful at all.

Following Bergman's instructions, she looked down as she walked in the door. A few seconds later, with her heart thundering in her chest, she lifted her head slightly for a quick glance around. She could clearly see the faces of the people near her, but the rest were shadowy. The lighting in the shop was dim. In order to tell if Darrin was there or not, she was going to have to take off the sunglasses. Which felt like the only protection she had.

She took them off, folded them and slid them into her pocket. When her fingers brushed her phone, she realized that it provided her a perfect excuse to keep looking down. Plenty of people around her were staring at their phone screens.

She fired off a quick text to Harry: Haven't seen him yet.

He immediately responded with: Don't try to rush things. Stay cool.

Stay cool. As if she were cool at all to start with.

The line moved forward and she took another quick glance to her left, toward the tables and shelves filled with coffee-related items, some local artwork and craft items for sale. That part of the coffee shop wrapped around farther, past the service area, so she couldn't see the entire seating area all at once. She didn't see Darrin or anybody even close to his appearance. No blond, thirtysomething men with stylish clothes and a gaunt face.

What if Darrin had already seen her, recognized her and left? The thought of what he might do to Caleb made her stomach turn. And what about Jasmine? If Darrin had realized this was a setup, involving Jasmine's phone and her car and even her clothes, it would be obvious that she had cooperated. Once he knew she'd betrayed him, his fury toward her would be immense. And lethal.

Finally, it was Ramona's turn to order. She stepped up. "Did someone leave a note for me here?" she asked.

The barista, a young woman probably in her early twenties, raised her eyebrows slightly, looking confused.

"It's a long story," Ramona said. Obviously, she couldn't explain it all. She did her best to force a smile onto her lips. "A…friend said he would leave one here for me."

"Um, I'll check. What's your name?"

She was so nervous she started to give her real name and then caught herself at the last second. "Jasmine," she finally stammered.

The server called out to her coworkers nearby to ask about the note. One of them said that there was a note left by somebody roughly an hour ago. The employee disappeared through a side door behind the service counter and returned a few seconds later carrying an envelope. When he held it out, Ramona saw that it had *Jasmine* written on it with a small heart drawn beside the name.

Ramona took it, stepped out of line and then slid her phone into her pocket so she'd have both hands free to open the envelope.

I'm watching you. Don't be afraid. I just want to talk. Like we used to. But I don't know if I can trust you. Don't touch your phone. Keep your hands where I can see them. Take a seat near the back door.

Was he really here right now? Had he raced over here after Jasmine made her initial call this morning? Had the visits to the two other locations been a ruse to buy time and deter anyone who might be following her? Darrin had become good at planning, that much was clear by his ability to elude the police and bounty hunters. Maybe this was the final step of a plan he'd cooked up days ago. One that he'd set in motion by going to Valerie's house, threatening her and working in a twenty-four hour deadline. He would have known that would get a response.

She had to lift her face to see where she was going as she made her way toward the back door. As soon as Darrin saw her up close, he'd know she wasn't really Jasmine. And then what?

One step at a time.

She moved around the corner to the

seating that was hidden from view from the front of the shop. She didn't see him. All of the tables were full, but she did see a couple about to vacate a table near the back door. She waited for them to leave and then sat down.

The weight of the phone in her pocket drew her hand like a magnet. She so wanted to reach for it, to talk to Harry or at least text him. But she didn't dare. She tried to look around from the corner of her eye, searching for Darrin. Three different times, the back door opened and closed. Each time, she'd wait a few seconds and then carefully take a look. It was never Darrin.

Until the fourth time. When she looked up, her first thought was, *Not Darrin*. This guy was dressed in generic, baggy clothes. His hair was black and he wore glasses. It was a good disguise—good enough to fool her at first glance—but after a few seconds she realized it *was*

Darrin. She recognized the predatory gleam in his eye.

The anticipatory smile disappeared from his lips and she could tell the moment he knew she wasn't Jasmine. The predatory gleam in his eye switched to full-on hatred. Ramona froze in fear.

Before she could move, the back door swung open again and a man rushed in wearing a ski mask that covered his face. The gun in his bright blue gloves looked huge as he lifted it and pointed it at Darrin.

Darrin had already started to pull his own gun out of his waistband, but he was too slow. The masked man fired two shots. Darrin dropped to the floor. And then the masked man ran back out the way he'd come.

The sounds of screams and furniture being turned over filled the coffee shop as the shop's patrons scrambled to get out of harm's way and escape through the front. Ramona had gotten to her feet and backed away from Darrin and the masked gunman without even realizing she'd moved.

Stunned and confused, it took her a second to remember the phone in her pocket. But before she could even reach for it, Harry was already shouldering his way through the crowd of panicked people still trying to exit the coffee shop. Bergman and a couple of plainclothes officers with badges hanging from their necks rushed in behind him with guns drawn.

Harry saw Ramona first, and while the cops hustled to check on Darrin, Harry ran to Ramona. He holstered his gun and wrapped his arms around her so tightly that her face was shoved into his shoulder.

"Are you all right?" he demanded, still hugging her. "Are you injured?"

She could barely draw in a breath to answer, but this time it wasn't due to fear or asthma. It was the tight grip of a man who, it seemed, had dared to let himself care about her more than he wanted to.

"I'm fine." Her voice came out muffled because she was forced to speak into his jacket. And then she made a point of hugging him as tightly as she possibly could, so he'd get the message that she felt the same way about him.

The coffee shop patrons who hadn't left were already giving information to the officers about what had happened. They pointed toward the back door, the direction where the shooter had escaped, and they gave descriptions of the black clothing and mask he was wearing.

"What did you see?" Bergman demanded of Ramona, putting an end to her embrace with Harry. "Who was the shooter?"

"He was wearing a mask," she said. "And he didn't speak. I have no idea who he was."

In the distance she could hear the wail of approaching sirens.

"We'll start scouring the neighborhood looking for the gunman," Bergman said. "You did good." He patted Ramona on the shoulder. "Right now, I think you better get back to the ranch and stay out of sight until we catch the shooter."

Emergency medical personnel arrived to tend to Darrin. One of the officers stayed with them as they got him packed up and ready for transport. Ramona could hear the officer trying to get Darrin to tell him where he'd stashed Caleb Petrov. The other plainclothesman went out the back door with Bergman.

Ramona turned toward the door, thinking she and Harry were going to leave, too, when he reached for her hand and brought her in close for another hug. Finally, he loosened his embrace, but he didn't entirely let her go. Instead, he gazed down at her with those deep blue eyes.

Her heart fluttered and her stomach begin to twist itself into nervous knots.

She knew exactly what her problem was. She'd fallen in love with this man.

And she hoped he'd fallen in love with her in return. His actions seemed to indicate that he had…but she was still afraid that the next words out of his mouth would make it all fall apart—that he'd say he couldn't love her, that he wasn't ready. She understood why he was afraid to love and lose again. She couldn't imagine the heartache he'd been through. She couldn't help feeling empathy for him.

The longer he gazed wordlessly at her, the more she was worried that he was going to start emotionally withdrawing from her all over again.

Instead, he leaned forward. So, she leaned forward, too. And the next thing she knew, his lips were on hers, his breath mingling with her breath. The world around them, and all its threats and dangers, fell away. She felt warm and safe and delighted. Being in his strong arms felt like she was right where she was meant to be.

Finally, Harry pulled away. But not completely. He still held her hands as he looked into her eyes and said, "I guess we both know life can be dangerous." He let out a deep sigh. "I've stayed on the sidelines long enough. And if I'm going to take chances on getting my heart broken again, I want to take those chances with you."

Gratitude coursed through Ramona like a waterfall. Gratitude that so many prayers for Harry's healing had clearly been answered. And gratitude that this man she'd come to love so much had finally found a way to use the courage he relied on to take care of other people to do something for himself.

And for her. The strangest feeling of crystal clarity about her life overcame her, along with a sense of awe from all of the events required to bring them to this moment together.

"I love you," Harry said softly.

"I love you, too." Ramona felt her eyes start to burn, but she held back the tears. Instead, she stood on her tiptoes and planted a quick kiss on Harry's cheek. "Don't worry, big guy," she whispered into his ear, "I'll keep your heart safe."

Harry still had a slight smile on his lips as they walked back outside, hand in hand, toward Jasmine's car.

Looking over, Ramona spotted a familiar face. It took her a few seconds to figure out where she knew him from.

It was Alex, the property developer. The man who built the condos where Jasmine lived.

His hair was matted, as if he'd recently taken off a hat. And his cheeks were flushed, as if maybe he'd been jogging. He was tossing a daypack into the back seat of a car. And when he withdrew his hands, Ramona saw the blue gloves.

"It's him," she whispered to Harry. "Alex. He's the shooter!"

Harry disengaged his arm from Ramona's and walked up to Alex with a friendly greeting and a smile. And then in an instant Harry had Alex flipped facedown on the sidewalk with his hands cuffed behind his back.

Ramona immediately called Sergeant Bergman, who ran up in seconds to arrest Alex and cart him off to jail.

That evening, Sergeant Bergman took a few minutes away from his long list of duties and met Ramona and the staff of Rock Solid Bail Bonds at their office in town.

"I'm going to let you fill in your family members on what I'm about to tell you," Bergman said to Ramona as soon as he stepped into the office. "I'm a little short on time right now."

Ramona nodded her understanding, while Harry stood behind her with his hands on her shoulders. Now that he'd finally admitted his feelings to himself and to her, he was in for the long haul, no matter what. He had her back, always. He would protect her, always. And he wanted to make absolutely certain that she knew that.

Bergman gestured at everyone to sit down. Harry and Ramona moved toward the couch, while Martin and Leon each sat in a chair. Bergman dropped down into a chair, looking impatient and exhausted. Cassie handed him a mug of coffee and he offered her a rare smile. "Thank you."

"You're welcome," she responded before sitting down on the couch beside Ramona. "Now, what can you tell us?"

"Caleb Petrov has been rescued. He was treated at the hospital and released. He'll have some nasty-looking bruises for a while and he had to get a dozen stitches in his chin, but he should be okay. Apparently, his younger brother, whom I met at the hospital, had made the mistake of dabbling in drugs. But while I was there, he was promising his family that he'd start drug counseling immediately."

Thank You, Lord, Harry prayed silently while Ramona squeezed his hand.

"Darrin Linder and Alex Ferrano are already ratting each other out, each trying to get the best plea deal." An uncharacteristically bright smile crossed Bergman's lips briefly before he took a sip of coffee.

"It turns out you weren't the only person wearing a bulletproof vest while visiting the coffee shop," Bergman said to Ramona. "Paranoid Darrin was wearing one, too. So, he survived the shooting, though the gunshots did cause some impact damage. And just before he was wheeled into surgery, he told me that some of the funding for his criminal business had come from Alex."

"Alex? But why?" Ramona asked. "He was already successful developing properties like Jasmine's condo."

"I've had to listen to both Darrin and Alex," Bergman said. "And, of course,

I don't completely believe either one of them. From what I can piece together, it looks like Darrin was making good money selling heavy equipment, but he wanted more. He met Alex when he started dating Jasmine. He admired Alex's success, and eventually the developer shared his secret, which were the drugs he sometimes used to work nonstop and get ahead of his competition.

"Alex is one of those very rare individuals who could use the drugs now and then but still keep things under control. Darrin could not. He was immediately hooked, and he shared his discovery with Jasmine."

Ramona nodded. It made sense. Darrin changed so drastically and so suddenly. Jasmine had been vulnerable to anything that might help with the depression she'd battled for so long. What a blessing that she walked away from the drugs, and Darrin, when she did.

"Darrin was stunned by how much

money he could make selling the drugs. And then he somehow got the idea to diversify into selling guns. Alex fronted some of the money for that in return for a percentage of the receipts.

"In the midst of all this, Jasmine broke up with Darrin. He started to fixate on Ramona and her family as his biggest problem and the reason why Jasmine wouldn't take him back. His instability and recklessness got out of hand, and he got arrested for the first time in his life.

"He thought he could buy his way out of trouble, so as soon as he was out on bail, he set up his first big deal to sell the guns. That was when Ramona found him at the cabin at the Western Trails Resort. Chasing after her and trying to kill her in the woods afterward was an impulse decision. He sent his thugs to follow her the next day and grab her at the train trestle. He thought if he forced her to meet with him, he could scare her into butting out of his relationship with Jasmine—and intimidate her enough that she wouldn't testify against him for shooting at her in the forest."

"What about the fire trap in Bridger?" Harry asked. "How did Darrin know about that? Was he even there?"

"Alex happened to overhear Jasmine talking on her phone and telling someone that Ramona was heading up to Bridger. She didn't mention that you were looking for Darrin," Bergman said, directing his comment to Ramona. "But Alex knew Darrin was hiding out up there and warned him that you might be coming. Darrin set the fire trap. And fired the rifle shots."

"Why did Alex shoot Darrin in the coffee shop?" Cassie asked.

"He could tell that Darrin was spinning out of control. When Darrin murdered his accomplices, Alex decided things had gone too far. Alex was already worried about Darrin's criminal activities would get tracked back to him. He wanted Darrin out of the picture, but Darrin would not tell Alex where his new hiding place was.

"Alex knew Darrin's weak spot was his obsession with Jasmine, so he played that up and helped Darrin devise his plan. All with the intention of drawing Darrin out, killing him and putting an end to it all."

"And his plan almost worked," Cassie said.

The sergeant stood and Cassie walked him to the door. Leon and Martin grabbed their coats and headed out the door to go capture another bail jumper.

"Well, I guess this means the nightmare is over and life can go back to normal," Ramona said as she turned to face Harry, who'd remained by her side.

Harry stood there, holding her hands. He didn't want to let her go. Ever.

"I'm very happy these horrible events have finally come to an end, and that two dangerous men have been taken off the streets," she added. She looked up at

Harry with her beautiful hazel eyes. "But I'm also a little sad that I won't be staying at the ranch any longer. I'll miss seeing you every day."

Harry let go of her hands to wrap his arms around her. "I hear you did a good job mucking the stables, so I'm sure you'll be welcome at the ranch anytime. And you'll be seeing a lot of me for as long as you want to." He loosened his embrace and went back to holding her hands. "And as far as life going back to *normal* is concerned, you can pretty much assume that's not going to happen. Not after you've gone and gotten yourself hooked up with a bunch of bounty hunters."

Seven months later

Ramona took a deep breath, blew it out, and then leaned back against the broad, muscular chest of her brand-new husband.

Harry, who was standing directly behind her, wrapped his arms around her waist and drew her even closer toward him.

Her heart swelled with joy.

The happiest day of her life was heading toward evening. She and Harry were at Kitchen Table, finally taking a moment to relax and enjoy their wedding reception. She'd been a little hesitant to suggest the diner as the location for the post-ceremony event, but by that time, Harry had tasted just about every kind of pie Eric could bake, and he was thrilled by the idea of wedding pies instead of a wedding cake. "Everybody loves pie," she'd told him. And he readily agreed.

Having all of her family and friends come here to help them celebrate just made sense. This diner was her home away from home. It had been for a very long time. And it was where she wanted to focus her work energy. Among the many things she'd eventually realized after having her life endangered was that she was exactly the person she was intended to be. Of course, she was a work in progress, like everyone else, but choosing the simple life of working in the diner rather than the corporate world was right for her. And ultimately, her parents agreed.

The afternoon wedding had been held at the church Ramona's family regularly attended. Several of her relatives who lived on the coast had made the trek east to be there.

Harry's family had been warm and inviting from the moment he first introduced her to them. His sister and a couple of his cousins had done a beautiful job decorating the church with the autumn harvest colors Ramona loved. Everybody from Rock Solid Bail Bonds plus everyone from North Star Ranch had been in attendance, and it was a remarkable sight to see them all so dressed up.

Harry had asked his dad to be his best man. Ramona asked Jasmine to be her maid of honor.

Ramona smiled at the sight of her cousin, dressed in a pale copper-colored dress, walking around with her head held high, chatting and making sure everyone felt comfortable. Staying sober and working on nearly lifelong emotional issues wasn't easy, but her cousin was proving it could be done.

From behind her, Harry leaned forward and pressed a kiss to Ramona's cheek. Followed by several more. "Considering the extreme conditions that brought us together, I'd say things turned out pretty well," he said.

People thought her husband was brave because he chased bad guys. But Ramona knew it also took real courage for him to be willing to love again.

She turned so that she was looking over her shoulder and planted several kisses on her husband's cheek.

And then she turned around for a *real* kiss.

Sometimes you're at a dark bend in

the road and you can't see forward to the light. But it's still there. You think you've lost everything, that you can't let yourself hope again because the pain of opening your heart again is too great. But the day will come when you can.

That's one of the many blessings of faith.

* * * * *

If you enjoyed this bounty hunter story
by Jenna Night,
be sure to read her
bounty hunter novella,
Twin Pursuit,
in the anthology Colorado Manhunt.

Available now from
Love Inspired Suspense!

Dear Reader,

Thank you for joining the chase and reading the first book in my Rock Solid Bounty Hunters series. I hope you enjoyed it. There will be two more books with bad guys to be captured, faith to be strengthened and love to be found.

Working through deep grief, like Harry has to do, is a tricky process. Suffering a profound loss in your life is certainly not something that you ever "get over." But if you press on in faith, one small step at a time, the day will come when you realize you can live with that experience and you're able to ease back into the flow of life. Things do get better and there's a path ahead for you. That path can be a good one, even if it isn't the one you imagined you'd be following. I have firsthand experience with this and I know it's true.

I invite you to visit my website, JennaNight.com, where you can sign up for my mailing list. You can also find me on my Jenna Night Facebook page. My Twitter handle is @Night_Jenna. My email address is Jenna@jennanight.com.

I'd love to hear from you.
Jenna